TALES
FOR
LATE NIGHT
BONFIRES

G.A. GRISENTHWAITE

Tales for Late Night Bonfires

STORIES

Freehand Books acknowledges the financial support for its publishing program provided by the Canada Council for the Arts and the Alberta Media Fund, and by the Government of Canada through the Canada Book Fund.

Freehand Books
515–815 1st Street SW   Calgary, Alberta   T2P 1N3
www.freehand-books.com

Book orders: UTP Distribution
5201 Dufferin Street   Toronto, Ontario   M3H 5T8
Telephone: 1-800-565-9523   Fax: 1-800-221-9985
utpbooks@utpress.utoronto.ca   utpdistribution.com

Library and Archives Canada Cataloguing in Publication
Title: Tales for late night bonfires : stories / G.A. Grisenthwaite.
Names: Grisenthwaite, G. A., 1959– author.
Identifiers: Canadiana (print) 20230454143 | Canadiana (ebook) 2023045416X | ISBN 9781990601378 (softcover) | ISBN 9781990601385 (EPUB) | ISBN 9781990601392 (PDF)
Classification: LCC PS8613.R646 T35 2023 | DDC C813/.6—dc23

Edited by Jamie Tennant
Book design by Natalie Olsen
Author photo by G.A. Grisenthwaite
Printed on FSC® certified paper and bound in Canada by Marquis

To all the old men (young men, and women)
who stand around backyard bonfires and
trade stories and laughter late into the night.
Where would we be without all y'all?

TALES
FOR
LATE NIGHT
BONFIRES

Splatter Pattern

Anyways, a kid, a boy, in town, drags his sorry halfbreed ass up Main Street — Only Street's what most of us call it — carrying on him the kind of sad that attracts rain like a pile of crap attracts flies. So that kid, the boy, wading in sadness, walks Only Street. Rain falls around that kid, the boy, all the time. Wades in sadness, we guess. Maybe wades in sweat-like rain.

Could be in an Elvis song that kid, the boy, living in "Heartbreak Hotel." Now that Elvis gets himself a co-writing credit on that song.

"Heartbreak Hotel" makes suicide a groovy thing. But that kid, the boy, don't think that-a-way.

No, that kid, the boy, got himself so locked up he don't see them thoughts, don't hear them brain words, can't speak none of it neither. Anyways, that father says only cowards make suicide.

Only one says jumping off the bridge'll make him better. Even heal him.

3

That one, Me-Who-Looks-At-Me, comes from spirit world maybe? Come from all the bad stuff growing in that kid's, the boy's, heart, maybe? But we don't know for sure. Anyways he says that boy's father lies and doesn't want him to get better.

Sure, we hear them rumours and sometimes screams from the house. Sometimes crying, that kid, the boy, in alleys, under stairs, in the public toilet. Probably at the house too; makes sense, i'nit?

We know something ain't right about that father.

But we don't know nothing but the rumours.

Father says to us, "You got no clue how clumsy and stupid and weak that kid. Lemme tell you. Just last night, that clumsy kid, just tying its shoelaces. They fall off a stool. Just fall off a goddamn stool and break a fucking wrist.

"Musta got all that weak from the mother, that kid. Musta got all that stupid from the mother, that kid. Musta got all that clumsy from the mother, that kid."

We think that kid's, the boy's, mother pretty smart to up and leave that father. Pretty cruel to leave that kid, the boy, behind, but.

When we ask that kid, the boy, "What happened?" he tells us, "O, just clumsy me. O, just weak me. O, just stupid me." Shrugs and sloshes away that kid, the boy. Sloshes away like that turtle with the head inside the shell. Rain splatters down. Wind catches it and spritzes our air with grey spray.

Wet footprints stain the ground behind him.

So few words we think maybe that kid, the boy, wrong in the head.

Maybe not enough oxygen inside the mother?

Maybe they drop that kid, the boy, on his head?

Maybe?

Who knows. We're not shrinks.

And we're not doctors.

Maybe?

Who knows. We got our own stuff to worry about.

Anyways, this story ain't about us. This story tells about Me-Who-Looks-At-Me, someone that kid, the boy, coulda made up. But Me-Who-Looks-At-Me tells us he made up that kid, the boy. Me-Who-Looks-At-Me steals that kid's, the boy's, dreams: night dreams; day dreams; dreams inside dreams; dreams inside the brain pictures behind the words that kid, the boy, says out loud. Me-Who-Looks-At-Me rules dreams. Me-Who-Looks-At-Me the warrior, qéck looking out for the younger brother. Me-Who-Looks-At-Me's born way after that kid, the boy, but already older. Way, way older.

Maybe more agile, stronger, and smarter, too.

That kid, the boy, wades up Main Street just before dark. And splosh-splersh by us. We say, "Hey."

Rude one, that kid, the boy. Splosh-splersh. He shrinks and throws up a wave like a block, splosh-splersh, like we take a shot at his head. Splosh-splersh. Water splat like a hawked loogie on the ground in front of us.

Splosh-splersh.

That kid, the boy, so rude.

Splosh-splersh down Only Street.

And that pick-up zooms over the hill.

So fast all four wheels clear its crest.

Truck rocks left, jerks right.

Straightens out.

And guns it.

Like it needs to go faster through town.

Like they got a lightning bolt up that tailpipe. And maybe gonna jump into some future.

Like it wants to splat that kid, the boy all over the street.

Only that kid's, the boy's, father drives that pick-up. And that's who's driving it.

That kid, the boy, stops right in the middle of Only Street. Right on the faded white line. He's got plenty of time to get offa Only Street. And just ten feet from the sidewalk he stops dead. Frozen stiff: maybe from fear, we think.

You know we want to say something.

You know we want to save that kid, the boy.

But we, frozen as him, wait and watch.

That pick-up don't hit the brakes. It swerves around them.

That kid, the boy, now split in two. That second one, Me-Who-Looks-At-Me, got a rifle: bolt-action .303.

They pull back bolt.

Kickback knocks them on their arses.

Oncoming headlights shine through windshield blood and brain splash-pattern.

Now we give our head a shake. And eyes a good rub. Did we just see what we see? We dreaming? That kid let Me-Who-Looks-At-Me kill their father?

Sure, that father maybe not the best, but to kill it like that?

Me-Who-Looks-At-Me jumps to his feet and hands the rifle to that kid.

That kid flicks the safety. Points its barrel down. Someone's shown them how to hold the gun when not killing with it.

Probably their grandpa.

That Me-Who-Looks-At-Me claps their hands, looks at us and says, "One helluva splatter pattern, huh?"

He grabs that kid by the sleeve.

"Gotta be one crazy exit wound! S'go check it out."

That kid feels empty to us. Like an old shell. We see that sometimes, soul or whatever check out and go on a TC, cruising Only Street. Maybe all zoned out?

Who knows.

Absence seizures, maybe?

We're not doctors.

Me-Who-Looks-At-Me skips to the truck. That father hunched over steering wheel like a sleeping drunk, don't move, even when Me-Who-Looks-At-Me poke it with a stick.

Pretty quick them cops show up.

Pretty quick they jump that kid.

Got him face down in the asphalt.

Big splash of water gushes from that kid. Sounds like them old ladies who cry at funerals.

One cop says, "Fucking kid pissed on me."

One cop says, "Dirty little Indian puked on me."

That kid now in the cop car, hunched over like that father.

That Me-Who-Looks-At-Me? Long gone.

One cop says, "Tell me what happened here."

We say, "We dunno. I guess someone shot that kid's old man."

One cop says, "Old man?"

We say, "You know, the father."

One cop says, "You seen it?"

We think a bit. No right answer. Cop probably wants to hear us say what he thinks we should say. Cop won't hear about Me-Who-Looks-At-Me. We can't blame them, can we? Cop makes us accessories for saying truth.

Seen it happen before.

Truth might let some free, but it imprisons many more.

Not always that way. But that way now.

Anyway, that kid will wind up in jail sometime. Jail, or dead. So no need to take us with him.

We say, "Yeah. Didn't know that kid had it in them. They usually so quiet. So shy. So pleasant. Don't know what went wrong. Pretty sad, hey?"

ball lightnin

she, maybe three, I guess
        no, four she was, down Cisco
        over there on the west side
  wearing her shiny shoes and Sunday dress
  for pickin berries? jeez you, says her gran
  better keep it clean, or that Sunday school god'll gechoo
  and she cackles
        you know the one, that old lady laugh?
  but she don't make her change
  so yeah, she meant to keep it clean
        anyways, I guess she tried
  walkin the CP track with her gran
  her gran and aunt and her stupid dog
  over there, on the west side
  at Cisco

near that place Fraser finishes swallowin Thompson
        where them two rivers, one all green and sparkly
    and the other all dirty, them two rivers roll into one
the three a them and that stupid dog
just comin back from pickin sx̱ʷúsm
yeah, sx̱ʷúsm, and wild raspberries, too
        anyways, them three and that dog returnin home
her gran haulin a basket a sx̱ʷúsm
and her auntie, a pail a raspberries
and that little one chasin that dog a hers
that dog runnin, in a jingle dress made a burrs
and she, that little one? got a smile
as stained as her fingertips
and that dog?
yippin up a storm
tail high and waggin, tongue lollin
she races up and back along the tracks
up and back, up and back
then this last time she runs up and up and up
tail folded up under her belly
paws barely touchin them ties
leavin them two-leggeds to fend for themselves
so that girl, she stamps a foot on a tie
calls after her stupid dog that disappeared around a bend
and from behind her, maybe a hundred feet
maybe a little more, her gran shouts, *run!*

and that little girl?
> she turns, sees a fireball
>> ball lightnin, an electric tumbleweed
>>> rollin her way
>>>> and that girl?
>> she runs
> her gran and auntie screamin after her
> their berries bouncin off the gravel between two ties
> and them old women, all in one motion
> hike up their skirts and chase the lightnin
> chasin that little girl

up them train tracks that little one runs
> with that lightnin ball right behind her
> then that little one
> she zigs off the track
> and climbs that scrabbly hill
> till Moses' barbed wire fence stops her dead
> so down she slides
> kickin up dust and pebbles
> down the hill
>> her mouth twisted into a scream she don't let out
> or maybe can't
> and she crosses them tracks again
> jumps a patch a prickly pear
>> jumps that cactus all right
>>> but trips, tumbling down
>>>> rollin like that lightnin ball

poppin out a little cry each time her butt touches ground
and that lightnin chases after her like mad on a mule
and then that lightnin ball fizzles, sputters
spreads that stink a ozone
and dies in a thunderous *boom!*

well! then her gran scoops her up
wheezin and cryin and holdin that child close
and that little one's fancy dress?
all dirty, and torn
her fancy shoes all scuffed and dusty
and that girl cries
maybe more for them scuffed toes
and that torn an dirty dress
than that fireball nearly takin her

her gran carries the girl tucked up under one arm
her basket a sx̣ʷúsm up under the other
and her aunt, now all thousand-eyed
watches the hill, the sky

them three hurry home
where that stupid dog's hid
under the house
hidin like a mole
they don't see her for maybe three days
yeah, three whole days
the whole time that girl cries

thinkin her stupid dog got ett by that fireball
thinkin maybe she got ett by that Sunday school god

three days she cries
then that dog?
her fur a messa caked mud and dust
her jingle dress a burrs
as runed as the girl's Sunday one
all whimperin, hungry
and she jumps up on that little girl
scaredy-tail waggin between her legs
forepaws on that little girl's shoulders
they hold each other
they hold each other tight
that little girl smilin a rainbow

and that stupid dog?
she tries lickin it off

Roadkill

Chuckie thought the two most important women in his life hated each other; well, Edna was a woman, and the other, Hazel, a '61 Impala ss. Edna despised Hazel, but Hazel couldn't hate Edna or anyone else. All 409 cubic inches of her engine loved her two-leggeds, even when she thought Edna a bit burdensome at times. But Hazel, as white as a polished pearl, and as smart and faithful as a purebred Arabian, loved Chuckie the same way she loved the caress of clean thirty-weight oil on her pistons.

Every now and then Chuckie took a drink; sometimes he took many. When Chuckie had too many, Hazel drove her man and his gang of rowdies home — and only home — no matter where her human charges thought they wanted to go. And Chuckie — drunk, sober, or somewhere in between, like tonight — chuckled and caressed Hazel's steering wheel like his lover's earlobe, and said, "You taking us home to bed, old girl?"

When Hazel pulled to a stop in front of the house, Edna, un-asleep in bed, relaxed, and as her head nestled into the pillow, snored lightly.

Her worried frown softened into a less worried one.

Despite his buds' cussing and grumbling, Chuckie, he all soft words and sledgehammer-fists, laughed, sent them on their way. "Catch you for coffee at Rose's in the mornin?"

His buds waved yeah, and grumbled up the rez road, yelling at yipping rez dogs, who now barked louder, and tried to shake free of their chains.

Chuckie leaned against Hazel's right front fender: "You could teach them a lesson or two, i'nit, girl?"

After the last of his buds closed their doors to the night, Chuckie nodded. He crawled into bed beside Edna. Her sleep breathing slowed and her less frowny frown smiled, looking kind of heavenly.

Some nights later, while tootling east on a narrow, curvy section of the Canyon (*Ah, Heaven! Wind through my grill at seventy miles an hour!*) —

Crash!

Thunk!

Thud-Thud.

Thud-Thud.

Thud-Thud.

A four-point white-tailed buck bounced off Hazel's right front fender, and landed on the shoulder, more dead than alive.

Chuckie saw a huge dent in Hazel's fender, new paint and trim, at least three hundred dollars in parts, and another year's delay in buying that new gas-powered log-splitter.

Edna saw a freezer full of venison roasts, burgers, jerky, and a hide and sinew for her crafts.

So did Hazel, not that she wanted any of it for herself.

"Put it out of his misery, then into the trunk. Hey, hun?" Edna said.

Chuckie, already reaching into the glovebox for his skinning knife and nodded. "On it, Sweet-thang."

He frowned at Hazel's dented fender, thanked her, thanked the buck, dragged it up beside that rock that looked like Coyote humping his sister-in-law, and then slit its throat.

Hazel's 409 rumbled to life. She rolled to a stop alongside Chuckie and the dead buck. He heaped the buck onto Hazel's dented fender, and dangled his head over its edge. The buck bled down Hazel's side. Its blood pooled at her whitewalled wheel. While the buck bled out, Chuckie made room for him in Hazel's trunk.

A ways down the highway behind them, Constable Macpherson shut off his cruiser's headlights, and idled to a stop.

He thought himself tricky, sneaking up on them.

But Chuckie heard him sneaking up.

And Edna heard him sneaking up.

And Hazel heard him sneaking up.

Hazel tooted her horn. Chuckie bonked his head on the trunk lid. He said, "Oww! What the ...?"

Edna said, "Talk to your damned car. That bitch got a mind of her own."

"Don't call my baby names. You know she don't like all that rough talk."

Hazel thought *bitch* meant female dog. So when Edna called Hazel *bitch,* she heard *Bitch,* the same way she heard Chuckie call her *Baby.*

"O, I'm so-o-o-o-o-o-o sorry! But she scared the living piss outta me."

Gravel crunched behind Chuckie.

That cop couldn't walk silent on a cloud, i'nit?

Chuckie grabbed the sixteen-ounce ball peen hammer.

And spun around.

That hammer was no match for that cop's drawn revolver, but if he'd left it holstered, one good pop with the peen and so long, copper.

Now face-to-face with that cop, a large man. And that large cop like a rabid weasel.

That rabid weasel cop, Constable Macpherson, thumbed the holster's security strap and said, "What you plan on doing with that hammer?"

Chuckie gently tossed the hammer behind him.

It landed with a dull clunk in Hazel's trunk.

Chuckie smiled. "Thought a bear'd sneaked up on me."

Edna scooted from the car.

The door chuffed closed, and Macpherson shot her a rabid-weasel glare.

The buck's bleed had slowed to a trickle: a thinning, steady flow, drizzling down the dented fender. Edna jammed the buck's rear hooves inside the windshield wiper well. Scooched up beside it. Held its front hooves in her lap.

Held them pretty tight.

Macpherson counted three:

the woman? no threat

the man, big, but pudgy? medium threat

behind the wheel, unknown?

Unknown, so potentially high threat.

Macpherson said, "You in there. Shut your motor off, and step out of the vehicle."

Hazel revved, "Vroom."

"Vrooooom."

"Right now."

He released the security strap holding his revolver. "Now."

"Vrrooooooooom." And she chided, "I'm not angry, frothing two-legged. Just playing with you."

And Chuckie coughed to hide his chuckle.

"Vroooooooooooooom." Puffs of black smoke shot from Hazel's dual exhaust.

Chuckie sniffed the air, and thought: "Hmm, the old girl's runnin a little rich. Better tune er up."

And Hazel said, "Who you calling old, Grandpa?"

Macpherson pulled his revolver and pointed it at Hazel's rear window.

Chuckie slid between Macpherson and Hazel. "Whoa there. Just hold on a sec. Ain't no one in the car. Look for yourself."

Macpherson squinted.

He stepped around Chuckie.

Macpherson extended his revolver.

He saw no one in the driver's seat.

Macpherson blinked.

Still saw no one in the driver's seat.

Hazel clutched into first and lurched forward a few feet. Edna said, "ʔÚu! ʔÚu!" She leaned into the windshield. She prayed. She slapped a hand into the windshield wiper well, fumbling for a finger hold. The buck's four points tappity-tapped like loose valves.

Tappity-taps around Hazel heeby-jeebied Chuckie. Chuckie held his breath and listened: "Nope. Them ain't Hazel's valves tappin."

Despite what Macpherson's eyes saw, he tapped on the driver's-side window.

He'd lived through World War II and the Korean police action.

Nothing shook him.

Nothing.

Macpherson thought, "Nothing gets to me. I've seen it all."

But he'd never seen a driverless car.

And he'd never seen a haunted car.

Macpherson thought, "Naaaaah. No such thing as haunted cars. Haunted anythings."

But his jaw and revolver hung limply as that driverless car drove away from him. Real casual. And not too fast.

Hazel stopped a little ways up the road.

Stopped long enough for Edna to slide off the hood and drag the buck into the trunk.

Edna didn't drive. She never needed to. And Hazel liked it that way. *Preferred it.* Hazel only did one thing and she did it well: driving. She probly could do more. But as a '61 Impala ss, driving was enough. Driving and looking damn fine doing it.

Edna slid into the passenger seat and patted the dashboard. Hazel eased onto the highway, then sped up the road about a mile and a half.

Stopped.

Edna dragged the buck up the path, leaving a trail behind her that would take a year to go stale.

Hazel popped herself into first and sped up the highway.

Six miles.

Hazel glided to a stop, killed her motor, and waited.

"Don't feel bad," Chuckie said. "She'll do that sometimes. She just get mad and drive off like that."

Macpherson, holstering his revolver, said, "Where you going with the roadkill?"

"S'not a roadkill. I killed him." Chuckie extended his hands, palms up, fingers splayed.

"Hunting out of season, drunk driving, possession of stolen goods, mischief: these charges, and any others I can think up between here and the lockup, are the charges you face, Mr. Bible."

"I killed that buck on our land. You can't arrest me for that."

"This highway is on Her Majesty's land. You killed the Queen's buck."

"It's my buck. I killed him on our land. See that rock there? The one looks like Coyote humpin his sister-in-law? Our territory begins there, so I got him fair and square."

Macpherson shone his light on the rock Chuckie pointed at.

"It's just a rock, Mr. Bible. And it too sits on Her Majesty's land. Irregardless, deer season's done."

"Maybe for you, but we got the right to hunt to feed ourselves. Anyways, we're standin on Indian land. Check your map."

"I don't need to check anything. What you call your land belongs to Her Majesty. You, as a ward of the Canadian Government, are only granted use of it. My job is to protect what's rightfully Her Majesty's."

"Don't being a ward mean your queen owns me, too?" Macpherson snarled.

He secured his revolver.

Macpherson handcuffed Chuckie.

He shovelled him into the backseat of his cruiser.

Macpherson fired up his cruiser.

He beetled off after the renegade woman, the renegade car, and the contraband deer.

They sped past Edna's trail, and Chuckie smiled into the cruiser's rearview mirror. Macpherson growled and back-handed the mirror, knocking it free of its mooring. It thunked off the passenger door.

Macpherson said, "Wipe that smile off your face, Mr. Bible."

And he said, "Bible, you're in big, big trouble."

He flipped on the cruiser's lights and siren, gripped the wheel, spanked the cruiser into overdrive, and drove.

Hazel slipped into neutral, just in case the cruiser bumped her rear-end. The cruiser screeched to a halt; its front bumper kissed Hazel's left front whitewall.

Macpherson blazed the spotlight on Hazel.

He shone his flashlight everywhere but up her tailpipes.

Macpherson found no keys in the ignition.

He saw no signs of mechanical tampering.

Macpherson saw no signs of life.

She seemed to be nothing but a '61 Impala ss. He poked the dark bushes with his flashlight's beam. Wind stilled, allowing a blanket of silence to suffocate Canyon.

Macpherson's neck prickled.

Sweat beaded his forehead.

He scuttled back to his cruiser.

Macpherson slammed the door closed, and slapped the door latch down. Chuckie smiled into his shoulder. And closed his eyes to hide it.

Macpherson pulled a U-ie, and cruised back to town.

While Macpherson checked Chuckie into the lockup, Edna, at her and Chuckie's fish camp, dressed out the buck, hung it from the old maple tree, sent a little prayer to Chuckie, made an offering for their buck, thanked Hazel, built a fire in the wood stove, then fixed a small batch of bannock. She brewed a pot of strong black tea. She plopped a can of SPAM® into a mixing bowl, added three shakes of Tabasco®, five squirts of Worcestershire sauce, and ground the mixture into a smooth paste, and then slathered some of it onto a piece of steaming bannock. After her meal, she fell into a fitful sleep on their lumpy old cot.

Hazel pulled into a parking stall beside the police station. She revved her 409 three times, and then shut herself down.

Chuckie curled up on the cell's cold, cement floor. He smiled, then drifted into a peaceful sleep.

Three Bucks

Chuckie, Alistair George, Miracle Johnny, Harold Billy and some others stood around Alistair's bonfire one night. Drinking tea, mostly. Maybe a little whiskey in one or two of them mugs. They'd traded stories all night. Each man shared his best hunting story. Miracle Johnny, almost as good a hunter as Chuckie, didn't tell stories nearly as good as Chuckie's.

"This one time I went out. Just me, my three-o-three, a box of shells, and a flask of whiskey."

Old Harold, all screwed-up face, says, "You didn't take water with you? Into that country? Even I took water with me when I went up them hills."

Sure, Old Harold had taken a lot of water with him, but he only drank from the jug of wine he kept under a blanket in the bed of his pick-up. But that was them days and them days had long since passed.

Old Harold didn't hunt or fish any more. Cos he got cataracts.

———

And rheumatoid hips. And them shakes. And you know you can't bait a hook when your damn fingers got them pa-pa-palsies.

Miracle nodded. "Well, when I go up into them hills now, I take a lotta water. Only water. And I'm gonna tell you why."

Miracle never started a story in a way that made you want to stop and listen. Chuckie topped up everyone's tea. Harold cradled it for a moment before gulping down three, five mouthfuls. Old Harold always said he needed a bellyful of wine to feel normal. Old Harold thought everyone needed a bellyful of wine to feel normal. Bellyful of that Jesus blood. Bellyful of that holy goodness.

But after Old Harold got them yellow eyes, smʔém said no more wine. Doctor said no more wine. So Old Harold whined, but didn't touch it now.

Old Harold quieted. Alistair quieted. Chuckie quieted. Even the fire stopped crackling. Chuckie sometimes waited before telling the rest of his story. So Miracle waited.

And waited.

Then. "This one time I go into the bush behind Gregory Abbott's. You know the one? Anyways, thick bush sometime. Not now. Fucking clearcut two hundred yards in.

"One time, thick forest for days. Not so much now.

"Heard about a five-point white-tailed up that-a-way. So I go up. See for myself, hey? Don't take long to pick up his trail. Fresh scat, maybe an hour ago. Maybe two. Stalking him so quiet I catch two bull snakes humping. Never heard me coming. Hey-hey!

"About noon now. And so hot them snakes is sweating.

"Sweat just pouring outta me. My gonch feels pissed in, hey."

26

Alistair said, "Making a swimming hole for your spaeksʔ, i'nit?"

Chuckie said, "More like a sauna."

Alistair said, "Nah, more like a sweat bath, i'nit?"

Sweat bath. Now that's a good one.

"Anyways, still not getting any closer to him, and I'm thirsty. So I take a snort of whiskey. Before you know it, no more whiskey. Them last few drops stick like a stain to the bottom.

"Still thirsty, but. And now sweating so much. Like someone shoved a garden hose up my ass, and used me as a sprinkler.

"Now, dizzy.

"So dizzy I got to sit. Flop. No shade. Fucking clearcut. No shade anywhere. Fucking clearcut.

"Little Creek usta run through here, from a spring.

"No more.

"Fucking clearcut.

"Still three miles to Johnson Creek, nearest water. Johnson Creek now. Was ʕlíyx. Now Johnson.

"So time kinda stop. Can hardly hold up my head now. Like too much drink in me. Or bad meat. But no cramps. No qʷnóx̣ʷenek.

"Mouth dry. World all blurry. Felt that way before, fighting in Korea. Got the malaria. And nearly die over there. Malaria just about kill me.

"Not Chinese bullet. But malaria.

"But no qʷnóx̣ʷenek. Just sweat. Lotta sweat.

"So, I'm dead soon. Say goodbyes. Húṁeł smʔém. Húṁeł Jaws. Gonna miss that mutt Jaws, hey?

"Say syémit. Ask xeʔłkʷúpiʔ keep them safe.

"Then laugh, hey?

"Laugh. If only I had a box of ċált to pour on me. Keep them sméṁix off, hey? Laugh. Old Indian drying like a rack of sċwén. But no ċált.

"Anyways.

"Little while, maybe a long one — hey-hey — someone taps my shoulder. Tap-tap-tap.

"He goes, 'Hey: hey, Mighty Hunter, you're not gonna make it.'

"That five-pointer. Muzzle in my face. Maybe he tapped me with his coup stick — hey-hey."

So old Miracle heard that white-tailed talk.

No telling what you could hear when you stop and listen.

But there's more to Miracle's story. Listen:

"So that deer. Five-points in my ribs. Ten. You hear about it sometimes. Mad buck gores a guy. Kicks him. Front hooves. Not back ones like mules. Front ones. Kick-kick, kick-kick.

"If this how I go, I go this way. Gored by five-point white-tailed. But not gored. Buck says, 'Hang on, Mighty Hunter. Take you someplace cool. Someplace wet. Get you a drink of water. Cool down.'

"So I says to that five-pointer, kʷukʷscémxʷ. What else could you say but kʷukʷscémxʷ?

"Anyways, that five-pointer carries me across that fucking clearcut. Little kʷẏéłps here and there. Everywhere dried syíqm. More grass. Lotta dust. Lotta stumps.

"Ḱə́st that land. Ḱə́st.

"Little bumpy, that ride. That five-pointer, he covers ground fast. And soon that ride ends. In a place with lotsa shade.

Almost enough to cool you. And he brings me some water.
And I drink some. And I soak the head. And drink some more.

"And after soaking my head again, that five-pointer's gone.
Rifle's gone. Maybe he left it in the fucking clearcut. Maybe that
five-pointer took it. Maybe it dropped on the way. So I think
I'll sit in the shade till after sundown, till it gets a little cooler.
And then follow that five-pointer's tracks out. And maybe that
gun's right where it fell. Maybe where I dropped it.

"So I put my clothes on branches. And lay in that pool. All
naked, hey? And I don't care who could see me. And rest my
head on a smooth rock. And then I slept. In a real waterbed,
hey? Hey-hey hey! Slept till after sunset. And that head cleared
up. No dizzy-head. No blurry vision. And still no qʷnóx̣ʷenek.

"Still no five-pointer. Still no rifle. Them clothes dry now
and all crunchy, and ever stink-ed, but I put it on anyways.

"Never seen that buck again. Too bad. Got a nice rack, that buck."

Miracle smiled into the fire. He saved that story a good long
time.

Now it's out there.

Alistair said, "Mm. Good story."

Old Harold said, "Yep."

Chuckie said, "Holding out on us, i'nit, Miracle?"

Alistair said, "After that one of yours, Miracle, I don't want
to tell mine."

Miracle said, "Tell it. Now I real wanna hear it."

"I guess. Anyways, this one's another hunting story. Happened
just this morning. Went up past Reddix. On McCullough's range
this morning. So about an hour after sunrise, following that old

deer path. Seeing nothing. Not even new poop. Heck, not even old poop."

"Gwan," said Chuckie, "even the blind can see them old turds up that-a-way."

Chuckie poured himself another tea, topped up Alistair's. "Shit, man! You gonna make shit up, make it believable."

Miracle mugs, "Ayii! Even I seen turds up there. Old ones, maybe from before they chopped most of that bush down for range land."

"You don't have to listen, i'nit?" Alistair snitted. "Anyways, when's the last time you got up that-a-way?"

Now Old Harold chirped, "Long ways to go chasing a rumour, hey?"

So, even though Old Harold gave up hunting sometime ago. Arthritic trigger finger. Shook pretty bad, from them drinking days. But he loved good hunting spíləx̣m. He'd call bullshit if Chuckie didn't. Chuckie hunts up there, too. But a spot southwest of Reddix, cos Hazel, his '61 Impala ss, won't drive that road. Too hard on her undercarriage, she said. Don't want no rocks puncturing her oil pan, she said. Pretty whiny for a muscle car, Chuckie said.

But Alistair looked ready to go. So let Alistair finish his story.

"So, I got this feeling and think I should keep on it, even though it's a real old trail. You know that trail so old Wind don't follow it any more. But I go up it anyways. Gut says go, so I go. So, I hear a little noise, maybe a hoof scratching out a root. And sure enough, maybe a hundred yards ahead, a three-point muley. Sight them. Then . . .

"Bam.

"Got it. Right between the eyes. Down he drops. Dead.

"Then I shoulder the rifle. Grab a tag.

"Then up he pops. Like I never hit him at all, hey. So I lift the gun and shoot him again.

"Right between the eyes. Bang."

Right here, at this spot in the story, Alistair stops the story.

Dramatic pose.

Dramatic pause.

Maybe he paused a little too long.

He had a good story, all right, but don't know when to stop.

When to go.

Sheesh, so not so great at telling stories, that man. Anyways, he picked it up again.

"So excited, I drop the tag. Bend over. Pick it up.

"Dang buck's up again. Maybe that muley's Jesus. Can't keep a good buck down, i'nit?

"Third time. Now I put a third shot between its eyes."

While Alistair sips tea, let that sink in a bit. Three shots to take down that three-point muley.

Alistair said, "Ever see a moose get up with three 30-aught-06 rounds rattling its skull?"

Again Alistair paused. Again!

I don't know about you, but I wish he'd just get on with that story.

While we wait, you think there's anything left of that three-pointed muley?

Alistair hid behind that big enamel cup of his.

And quietly sipped his tea.

Chuckie liked to slow a story down as much as anyone.

He liked to give you time to think about what he's said. But even Chuckie'd had enough. "So, that it?"

Maybe Alistair forgot the end of his story. Sometimes it happened.

"No. I got the best part now. Got one in the chamber. It gets up again, it goes down a fourth time. Five minutes I wait. Ten.

"Then creep toward clearing. Nothing moving but me. Like I said, not even Wind visits that place. Maybe three yards inside the edge of it lays a three-point muley.

"Dead from a single headshot.

"Five yards past that one, a second three-point muley. Just as dead as the first one. Got a single bullet between the eyes.

"Two tags. Two bucks. First hunt of the season, and last.

"And then. Strangest thing I ever saw.

"There's a third three-pointer about five yards past the second one."

Miracle said, "You shot three different muleys within seconds of each other?"

"Nope. Four. Musta got him with the last shot."

Chuckie said, "They didn't scatter when the first one went down?"

"That's right."

"I call bullshit. Where's the fourth?"

Well, now that Alistair took his story a little too far. Even the best hunter would've stopped at one buck, maybe two. And maybe talk about the big one that got away, kinda like fishing tales with fur, hey?

So Alistair, "Maybe I shoulda started by saying I took the semi-automatic up there. You know how you squeeze a little too hard and that thing fires a three-round burst. I figure maybe them bucks caught them bullets and dropped dead before the sound of it hit their ears, hey?"

Chuckie, Old Harold, and Miracle shook their heads no. A hard no.

"Okay. Maybe I made up the fourth. Hadda make up that one, hey? Make the story better, hey? But check out the shed. See for yourself. It's curing in the shed."

Harold grumped, "Four bucks on three shots? Bah! Even stupid drunk, I woonta fallen for that one."

Chuckie said, "Gwan, Dead-Eye, show us then."

So true to his word, Alistair had three good-sized mule deer hanging in his shed, wrapped in cheesecloth. The room smelled like rotting blood and decaying meat. Big old freezer hummed in a corner. One or two moose meat steaks leftover from last winter still in that freezer. A couple of deer roasts. Some deer and pork sausage.

Lots of room for fresh deer meat. Lots of room.

Alistair said, after the men finished inspecting his bounty, "Hey, Miracle? I only got two tags. So you take one. Take one for your family."

"Kʷukʷscémxʷ. I'll pick up its tag tomorrow."

Chuckie said, "Want some help butchering it?"

Miracle said, "I could help too."

"More the merrier, hey?"

Harold grumbled, "I'd help, but my damn fingers, and damn knees woont let me."

You know both Miracle and Alistair said to themselves: "Gotta set aside a leg for Harold."

Alistair says, "I got to say, you had the best story tonight, Miracle."

Chuckie slapped Miracle on the back. "Yep. Good story. Yours, too, Alistair. Yours too."

Little Trees®

for my niece, Ryann

Used to be you tell someone you saw sċuwenáÿtmx and they'd
either laugh in your face, or ask where? when? how big? — you
know, them kind of questions. Only old Billy Alexander — the
Billy Alexander running the rez gas station, not the other one
they say's up to no good — never asks them sorta questions.

Old Billy Alexander asks only one question: So, how *is* the
old boy?

When old Billy had his sight — he's blind now — he trapped
up in the bush behind Johnny Pete's place. That bush behind
Johnny Pete's place disappeared faster than Old Billy's eyesight.
What them city-boy loggers left behind, that big fire in '76 ate
up. Sure, new growth rised up, but like a fifteen-year-old's first
moustache and so scarce even them ticks got nowhere to hide.

So one day Timothy Black screeches to a stop at the gas pump
and huffs and puffs into the gas station's show room: Simon says

he has a sċuwenáýtmx camping in the old white barn. And you know that Simon can stretch the truth a bit, i'nit?

So old Billy Alexander says, Hmm, probly that Stew. So how *is* the old boy?

And he has a smile on him like yesterday's washed into today and makes tomorrow. You only see a smile like that when some yéyeʔ looks at pictures of her grandkids passed too soon. Old Billy don't wait for an answer. He okay? Gimme a ride out there?

Like I said, it's up Simon John's. Inside that old white barn. You know the one needs a new roof? That old one, still standing? Dunno if he's okay. Haven't gone down there yet.

Simon John's old barn made it through three forest fires. You call them wildfires nowadays, but in them days forest fires. Over the years three forest fires, and one of them close enough to bubble the white paint on the west-facing wall.

Simon bought that paint to make his new barn white, but the guy at the hardware store said he can't sell white paint for barns on that side of the river. Simon says, As long as that damn Chuck Connors could play Geronimo in a damn movie, I can have a damn white barn.

That hardware guy, older than them Kendricks & Sons coffee grinders he got in that display window, damn near craps his drawers, mumbles something about rules, he's just following the rules. The old guy has a name, but no one says it, afraid saying it out loud might make their whole clan move here, and no one wants that.

No one.

The old guy mumbles, How can you afford this much paint all at once? You know you can't put it on a tab or on layaway.

Simon waved a fat wad a cash under the old guy's nose and said, When you ever let one of us run a tab here, hey?

Now that same old guy owns the grocery store too. He gived every family a fifty-dollar tab, and let them run it as long as they keep paying it down. But he wouldn't let you put ten cents worth of nails on a hardware store tab, even if you offered up your wedding band as collateral. Now don't ask how I know this, specially not when the wife's around, hey? Now Simon coulda squeezed that old guy's neck shut in one of his hands, but no. I guess he didn't want his family and friends to lose their tabs and whatever because of something stupid he done. Instead, Simon said, Whose damn rules?

That old guy mumbles, Not my rules. If you don't like it, take it up with the Indian Agent. Take it up with the government.

So Simon says, You could take my money, or you could leave it. Either way, that white paint comes with me. I got a red barn and I want it painted white.

That old guy counted out what he needed for that white paint, and said, They'll come and get you, Simon. Just you wait and see. Don't know what'll happen. But it won't be good, I'll say that much.

So, Simon folds a single and puts it in old guy's shirt pocket. He says, Kʷukʷscémxʷ.

He puts that white paint on his red barn. And he waits for them, the Indian Agent, the government, and the RCMP.

Twenty years later and them people still don't come.

Thirty years later and he still waits.

Anyways, Old Billy asks, He okay? It's Stew, hey?

Sometimes I think you're as deaf as you are blind, Billy. I already said I haven't gone down Simon's yet. He calls me on the telephone and says I need to tell you he has a sc̓uwenáy̓tmx in that old white barn.

So it sc̓uwenáy̓tmx named Stew then?

Couldn't say. Didn't ask. Like I say, third time now, I have yet to go down there and see for myself.

He stink?

When it comes to stink, stink's a nice word for Stew's smell.

Maybe Old Billy's too excited to know he asks nothing but silly questions right now. And Timothy smiles and nods. Sometimes he talks to Old Billy like he's one of his grandchildren.

Take me up there.

Who'll watch the station?

Ach. I'll just shutter down. Anyone who wants gas can get it at Shaw Springs, hey? Or they could wait.

Old Billy walks like a guy with arthritis in both knees and two working eyes. He pushes open the door to the diner and waves hey to Sam, Charlie, and Peter. Sam, Charlie, and Peter yak it up at their usual booth in the north corner. The three of them have their coffee, their trucker's breakfasts, and Charlie got that morning paper. He reads headlines and big city people's obituaries. He don't need a newspaper to know about deaths around here, and the ones he don't hear about he sees on the bulletin board outside the post office.

LITTLE TREES®

Sam and Charlie look up from their plates. Sam has a forkful a sausage at his lips. Peter has a triangle of toast oozing egg yolk hovering half a foot over his platter. Charlie looks over the top of his paper and says, Just read about a Canadian pioneer who helped build the country. Helped settle the land. Started as a scrubland farmer in northern Saskatchewan. Moved west to build the first fishing lodge on the West Coast and become the first man since James Teit to discover and anthropologize coast Indians.

The three of them say, yíʔa tek sinwénwen, Snəḿnəḿ. Sam and Peter wave. Charlie nods.

I guess they forget Old Billy's blind. Most people do.

Old Billy says, Hey, Sarah.

Sarah pokes her head out the pass bar window and asks, What's up, hun?

Going up Simon John's place for a bit. Maybe one hour. Maybe two. Hard to say.

In the middle of the day?

Ach, it early yet. No one'll miss me.

Anyways, Charlie says, from behind his newspaper, anyone wants gas, just feed them your bean soup, hey?

Sarah laughs.

Sam laughs.

Peter laughs.

Old Billy laughs.

It's good soup, that bean soup of Sarah's, but it make you bark like snkẏép if you eat too much.

So up to Simon's Old Billy goes. His nose and ears work

39

like his eyes used to. Old Billy sniffs the air. And he sees wet fields, drowning hay, skinny cows, and horses needing a good grooming and oats, maybe a carrot or two. As they bump along Westside Road, Old Billy mounts his old Indian Scout Streamliner. In his mind, his Streamliner breaks that other bike's world land speed record. Old Billy's Streamliner went like stink, but not nearly as fast as Burt Munro's.

Still, he relives them old days, in the wind. And Old Billy smiles, rattling along Westside Road, his head out the window. And you know, if Old Billy had a tail, it would beat against the seat in 7/4 time. And like it or not, Timothy Black starts humming "Jocko Homo," even as his brain argues whether Joplin's version of "Me and Bobby McGee" outshines Kristofferson's. Timothy Black has that argument every time he drives in the rain and he never sides with Kristofferson. Anyways, Timothy Black never listens to that New Wave weirdo music and the CBC would rather sever its tongue than play Devo. Maybe his kids play that Devo?

Dust like smoke roosters up and settles around Timothy Black's pick-up. The sign on Simon's front door says, USE BACK DOOR! Them words is double underscored.

Doubled.

Simon means business. They say you could get two barrels of rock salt you try going through that front door when Simon's home. Thing is, Simon don't care what door you use. But his smʔém Martha don't want you tracking dirt over her precious Persian rug. And best you keep your dusty boots off it.

And Old Billy bee-lines it to Simon's barn.

He only falls once, trips over a rake or something. One left behind by one of Simon's grandkids, probably that Perry, that one lives in a dream all day long. Dreams so much all day, he has none left at night. But that one worries Simon. Daydreaming on the rail gang, or green chain, or felling trees. And no way Perry ever work as choker man. Maybe not even drive a tractor on the farm. Who knows?

So, yeah, that Stew stinks all right.

Old Billy's eyes water — but he don't cry; he never cries. And his nose dries up and his lungs shiver in fear, kinda like the TB but not quite.

Old Billy cries different tears, too. Says, ʔÉxkʷ n̓, qéck! ʔÉxkʷ n̓!

Stew tears up too and says, Sínciʔ! Long time no see.

Yeah, been a minute, hey?

So they talk a long time, them two. Old friends with a lot of catching to do.

They laugh.

They smoke.

And Simon brings them tea.

And Simon brings them sċwén.

And Simon brings them bannock and wild raspberry jam.

Them one or two hours Old Billy closes that gas station? Now two, three days.

Now after five days, Old Billy's ears perk up. Sarah's truck stops maybe two hundred yards from the barn. It coughs and sputters, shakes and rocks. No matter what Old Billy tries, he can't keep that truck from running on.

Sarah stands at the barn door and says, Hey, old man. Time you got back to work, hey? People want gas.

Stew says, Feed them that bean soup of yours. And he laughs.

Sarah laughs.

Old Billy laughs.

Stew says, You know I love that bean soup you make. O, boy, your bean soup, now that's one good soup.

Sarah says, Just good? Everyone says it the best soup they've ever eaten.

Maybe the best soup for some. But mine's your French Canadian pea.

Old Billy snickers every time anyone says *French Canadian Pea*. That Grade Four brain of his still laughs at that silly stuff.

Sarah says, You come back to the house with us, Stew. You have a sweat bath and shower. Sweat bath and shower. Two times each, sweat bath and shower. You, too, my sx̱aẏwih. Clean up. Put on clean clothes. Then have a bowl of bean soup. Maybe a trucker breakfast too. Maybe chicken waffles. Then, you, my sx̱aẏwih, get back to work, okay? You have plenty of cars waiting for gas.

Simon says he will only get rid of Stew's stink by burning his white barn.

Old Billy says, Naaaaaaaah! It's a good barn yet. Fix that roof and you'll get another twenty, thirty years. Maybe more.

But that stink makes cows' milk all green. Funky.

Stew says, I'll fix everything after two sweat baths and two showers. Till then, you add a little red food colour. It'll make that funky milk funky *chocolate* milk. People will go crazy for it.

I'll sell it at the gas station. Sarah will put it on the menu. Big seller that funky chocolate milk.

Simon says he'll think on it.

Stew talks on and on and on about the forest not just disappearing, but forests gone. Complains about how hard it is to hide behind trees no bigger around than his thumb. To be fair, Stew has thumbs like that Sissy Hankshaw. But he makes a good point. Them trees make good toothpicks nowadays, maybe pretty good pulp for paper, but not good planks.

He says, How can sċuwenáy̓tmx stay mysterious when no matter how hard you try to hide, an elbow, or big, hairy butt stick out?

So Old Billy goes back to work.

Five days away and Astrid Johnny's already waiting at them pumps before Old Billy gets there at 4:30 of that sixth morning.

Been here waiting two goddamn days. Two days wasted, waiting for you.

You could've gone to the Esso out Shaw.

Nope. I never buy gas from a séme?, especially that one.

So you sat at my pump for two whole days?

I'm old, Billy, not stupid. Car has no gas, so I stay with my cousin Ruthie on the rez. Wait and check to see if you've opened up. Ruthie and me drink tea and gossip. Wait some more and I check to see if you've opened up yet. Then wait some more.

Well now your wait's over, i'nit? Check your oil?

And the tires too?

Sure thing.

A blind man reading the tire gauge? Naaaaaaaah, not really, but he makes pretty good guesses.

Old Billy thinks on Stew's puzzle a good long time.

He thinks on it so hard, sometimes he forgets to take money for the gas he pumps.

Sometimes that Astrid Johnny pulls up to the pump and honks the horn, drives over the bell hose over and over, and maybe cusses Old Billy out. Each time Astrid does that, Old Billy nods and smiles and says, ʔÉx kʷ n̓, Astrid. How you going?

(Old Billy listens to Australian shows on Netflix. He and Sarah especially like *Offspring*. What a wacky bunch that Proudman family.)

Most of them just pay Sarah. Some drive off without paying, thinking they that Bonnie or that Clyde.

After a long time, maybe six or eight days since leaving Simon's barn, Old Billy solves Stew's puzzle. Hey, qéck, you thought about losing weight? Maybe you trim a hundred pounds off your butt?

Old Billy laughs. Thinks he makes a good joke.

Old Billy cannot lie; he likes big butts. That's what makes his joke so funny.

But Sarah don't laugh.

And Stew don't laugh.

He waits till the sting of their scowls stops burning. Joking! Holy! But listen. How about you work graveyard shift here? You start May long weekend when the gas station opens twenty-four hours. It'll be busy, but not like the old days before that new freeway.

Before work every morning Stew showers.

And Stew has a sweat bath.

And Stew smudges after that sweat bath.

And Stew has another shower.

And Stew has another sage smudge.

Every morning Stew smudges two times.

His spirit all squeaky-clean and stink free.

Even after all that showering and bathing, Stew smells like northern temperate rain forest, all damp moss, mushrooms and toadstools, and rotting yellow and red cedar. His stink's not so bad now, but it still makes your eyes water and your nose itch.

Such a stink, that smell.

He combs his hair. He curls his beard and singes cheek hair with Sarah's curling iron. Stew thinks he looks just like that Jesus fellow. He puts on big Hawaii shirt. He puts on big dark glasses. Stew thinks that shirt and them dark glasses make him look like that Big Lebowski Dude.

But that Dude don't wear a big Hawaii shirt.

Maybe he confuses that Dude with that Detective Sergeant Andre DeSoto? No matter, because Stew says, That don't change how I *feel* in this big Hawaii shirt.

Stew might like it, but that shirt's so loud it hurts my ears.

Stew says, Hmmm. Good point that.

So Stew wears his fur. He wears them moose-hide moccasins Sarah's made for him. She uses most of one moose hide to make them moccasins, Stew's feet that big. Making them takes ten straight nights. His feet don't touch the ground; no, he hovers above it. Stew skates on air like that Bobby Hull fellow on a breakaway from centre ice. He skates through town so fast you can't say what you've seen, or if you've seen anything at all.

That's how fast Stew skates on air.

Stew gets to work at 10:30 and eats the meal Sarah puts out for him.

He eats out back, resting against a jack pine thicker than toothpick lodgepole pines in the hills he calls home. That smell of diesel and gas reminds him of home, too. So do food wrappers and other papers dancing in wind.

Dancing in dust devils.

All that dancing garbage reminds him of home.

Bottles and broken glass reflecting streetlight kind of remind him of home.

Back home that glass there don't shine at night.

If Stew don't watch his step, his big feet get slashed by all that glass. Too bad he don't have Sarah's moose moccasins then.

Stew wears a sticky name tag on his chest, on the left side: *Hello, my name is Stew.* He sits behind counter, watches the CCTV for shenanigans at the pump island, watches for shenanigans behind the building, watches for shenanigans in Sarah's diner.

The first night he works alone, no cars need gas. Old Billy stops by around four, with coffee and tuna fish sandwich for Stew. They tell stories till Old Billy has to start work.

Second night's same as first night.

Third night's same as second.

Finally, the long weekend comes and brings with it cars, tens of cars. First one's a woman in a Jeep CJ. Stew says that CJ's the last good Jeep ever made. She pays, her face screwed up, her lips pinched tight, her eyes tearing up. Stew knows that face, that light-a-match-damn-you face. The woman pumps thirty-six bucks worth of regular into her Jeep.

Small talk puts people at ease.

Small talk lays the groundwork for relationship building.

A happy customer is a repeat customer.

Stew's done his homework. So, he says, You have a great Jeep. She's a thirsty one tonight, i'nit?

She slaps down a fifty and runs for the door, shouting, Keep the change.

So much for small talk.

So much for relationship building.

A woman drives the second car and fills up. She opens door, fanning one arm across her face, other hand over her mouth. Stew thinks, Why all these women drive alone at night?

Stew think she says, Christ, did you shit yourself, or what?

Stew knows he looks like that Jesus fellow. Or what, he says. I wear that new Hugo Boss® called Mountain Musk. It's real popular around here. Also, I get a little nervous around beautiful womans.

Maybe she blushes a little. Hard to say. She don't breathe much, across from Stew like that. She pays with her credit card. She says, You better get over it because that nervous stink of yours is bad for business.

Stew points his lower lip at her as he nods. I'll take that under advisement. Kʷukʷscémxʷ, come again.

At four, Old Billy puts a salmon sub on counter for Stew. That sub's something else: a side of planked spring salmon with red onions, capers, coarse salt, in a giant loaf of French bread Sarah bakes just for that one giant sub. She makes salad from ċewete?, Boston leaf lettuce, and radicchio, with juniper berry vinaigrette. Ever fancy!

A good meal, that.

Old Billy says, You know, qéck, business ain't like them old days.

Stew stops chewing. He looks around, says good bye to tires and wheels on the wall, shiny now, cos Stew's dusted them and polished them: that red box of windshield wiper blades, shelves of 10w–30, 10w–40, automatic transmission fluid, little light bulbs in boxes, little light bulbs in hard plastic wrapping, big light bulbs – headlights – in boxes, that box of Sen-Sen beside the till, and that board growing flat little fir trees called Little Trees®. They look kinda like fir, maybe spruce, and smell kinda like pine, but the pine your bathroom kinda smells like, not the kinda pine that once grew in the bush.

Old Billy pats Stew's hand. I got ideas to make our business grow. Qéck, you wanna help grow business?

Stew asks, How?

Old Billy says, You know how every picture, moving or still, we get a sċuwenáẏtmx all blurry, or looks like a man in a monkey suit?

Stew nods, not sure he likes what Old Billy's about to say. Old Billy spends the rest of that night and most of that next day answering the how.

Old Billy pays Maggie Campbell to make a giant kilt and giant Scotch hat with giant white dingle ball on top.

Maggie corrects Old Billy, We call it a red tartan bonnet, or tam o'shanter. And for which clan?

Old Billy thinks a minute.

Then ten.

Old Billy's smart, but he don't make important decisions quickly.

Fifteen minutes later Maggie asks, You awake, old man?

O, yeah, still awake. Still breathing. Seems to me Sarah has a great-great-great-grandfather from Scotland. A prince from them Highlands, or something. McDougall? That name mean anything to you?

She nods, Aye, old time enemies of we Campbells, those McDougalls. But a prince you say? We dinna hae princes as such.

Old Billy shrugs, Well, that's the story she got.

She says, you dinna hae a right to a tartan belonging to any clan not your own.

But she agrees to make that giant kilt and giant red tartan bonnet because it's a McDougall tartan.

And Old Billy pays top dollar.

Ten weeks later the whole province buzzes with news about Scotsquash sighting. The CBC shows film with Sasscotch, big hairy beast wearing that McDougall tartan and McDougall red tartan bonnet tromping over meadows in south central British Columbia.

Meanwhile, back at the gas station, Stew wears them Little Trees® like Christmas decorations. That smell almost covers his natural one, his nervous one. People say he looks festive. Some people say he looks just like Scotsquash. Stew says, he gets that a lot, but he's no McDougall, so he don't wear that tartan.

Some say he looks a lot like Sasscotch. Stew says, I get that a lot, but I'm no McDougall, so I don't wear that tartan.

A little white lie helps the bottom line and no one really gets hurt. Hell, even that McDougall clan gets some good press.

Everyone nods and says, O, yeah. Now I can see it. You really don't look anything like that Sasscotch and you don't look anything like Scotsquash either.

Everybody nods and buys postcards from that new rack of postcards by the till, where the Sen-Sen once sat. The biggest seller has Sasscotch lying on top a wood pile. Looks just like that Burt Reynolds fellow in that *Cosmopolitan* magazine, but in kilt, and beard curly like that Jesus'. The next biggest seller got that Scotsquash wielding a huge two-headed axe near a wood pile stacked higher than him.

Stew wears them Little Trees®, and them Little Trees® make Sasscotch invisible, make Scotsquash a mystery.

People everywhere see Sasscotch on farms, hiding in barns. Other people see Scotsquash running across bald mountaintops flipping the bird at passing passenger planes. Same people see them every night at Old Billy's gas station.

Can't see Sasscotch through them Little Trees®.

Can't see Scotsquash through them Little Trees®.

And they sure don't see Stew standing in front of them.

Catching Farts

Now this story happens about thirteen years ago. Maybe more. It's the one about Yellow at four, and how he learns to bottle cow farts. Before you run off screaming for PETA or Child Protective Services, give it a listen. It might surprise you.

Maybe.

Maybe not.

Okay. Sometimes I tell this story with Edna in it. Edna loves Yellow like her own, if she'd had any. Sis will ask, "Where's Edna?" Cos she'd rather leave her boy Yellow with the both of them, if she has to leave them with her brother and his sm?eméče at all. See, Chuckie and Edna don't have kids, and Yellow, Sis thinks, challenges even skilled parents, better parents than her. So in that version of this story, Chuckie says, "Edna took her mom shopping down the Loops. They're gonna stay up Deadman's, at her cousin Lily's. Be back sometime."

And that's how this version of the tale starts too:

Sis asks, "Where's Edna at?"

"She took her mom shopping down the Loops. They're gonna stay up Deadman's, at her cousin Lily's. Be back sometime."

Anyways, the story goes like this.

Yellow, at four, had enough energy to fuel a sun. His mother loved her son as mothers do, but keeping him safe and busy exhausted her, leaving her as tired as a soldier who has quick-marched across Death Valley. Each morning that baby escaped his crib. And his mom, who loves him as mothers do, drags her tired butt and that bouncing baby boy to her brother Chuckie's place.

She cries into her Earl Grey with honey (and a two-finger-spritz of whiskey — the five-year-old stuff, no skimping here, not where his sister is concerned).

"So, Sis," Chuckie says, cos Sister is her name — nineteenth of nineteen children. Her parents and grandparents and great-grandparents had run out of names. Too tired. No one in all those generations has less than fifteen siblings. So Chuckie says he and Edna will only make babies if he can name them numbers. No one likes that idea. No one.

"Too soon?" says Chuckie.

Silence.

Chuckie had a number. Eighty-two was Chuckie's number. Not a good number. And an even worse year.

Anyways, Chuckie suggests stringing a coil of razor wire around the top of the crib, "Like you see in them prison movies," he says. Now Chuckie always ends his crazy-talk with a loud laugh, and when no one else joins in he goes, "I was joking, jeez you."

Don't wait for him to say it now.

Instead, he says, "Lookiiiiit. You need rest. The boy needs boundaries. Win-win."

"What I need's a day off. Maybe two."

"What you need's another tea. Whisktea and honey."

"Kʷukʷscémxʷ, but no. One's enough."

Now that they've stopped talking all you hear nothing, except Chuckie slurping his tea, the dull clunk of he and Sis's mugs hitting the table now and then.

A good silence.

Until you remember four-year-old Yellow wanders his uncle's house untended and unrestrained.

Yellow somehow has scaled Gran's 120-year-old wooden rocker, precariously balanced atop its back and reaching for the big glass bowl full of shotgun shells. His four-year-old brain knows the boom they make. He likes the boom. He likes the smell of the blue smoke guns fart after they boom. Why don't my farts make pretty blue smoke? Maybe, maybe-maybe. Maaaaaaybe I just need to munch-munch wunna them shot gun's candies. The explosion of glass, the pop of pellets piercing pop cans and plastic jugs makes him squeal and clap his hands. And dance a happy kind of pee pee dance. He likes that Uncle Chuckie will give him his own 12-gauge when he turns twelve. And loves that his mom will let him. Those two twelves make him laugh: twelve-gauge twelve. Words taste like gun smoke. I'll hip-shoot bad guys like that famous TV Indian Chuck Connors. Blam! Blam! I'll hip-shoot renegade Injuns? renegade Engines? like that famous TV Indian, that rifleman. Blam! Blam! Tricky

Injuns? Engines? And renegades look a lot like Injuns. But don't wanna shoot Indians.

I bet I know what you're thinking. Believe me. Everyone tries telling him the rifleman's a white guy called Chuck Connors.

Everyone.

"Nuh-uh," says Yellow, "no séme? could play Geronimo like that rifleman."

You know, his great-grandfather Beltran, who loves them old cowboy movies, went to his grave sorry he let the boy watch them with him. Old Beltran, near the end, said he kept watching them, hoping one day the Indians would win.

Here's the catch. Yellow's four-year-old mind doesn't fathom twelve, except that twelve is not tomorrow, and probably not next week, either. But them shotgun shells sit way up high on the big-people-only shelf and them shells smell like right now. Right now. This minute.

"You hear that?" Sis asks.

"What?"

Another mouse in the Corn Flakes?

Another family of raccoons in the attic?

An elk or white-tailed chewing new bark off the cherry tree?

Nope. And now Chuckie hears it too.

He hears *the quiet!* just as Sis says, "It's too *quiet!*"

Their mugs slam to the table as one.

As one they race to the other room.

As one their mouths freeze in an unyelled, NO.

How does a lumpy-drawered four-year-old boy stay atop an old wooden rocker without smashing his head on the floor?

How does that frail 120-year-old wood not splinter under his twenty-six pounds of nuclear energy?

That pesky Gravity asks them very same questions.

That 120-year-old wood rocking chair asks them very same questions.

Gravity stomps her foot: "I make the rules around here."

That 120-year-old rocking chair says, "I may be old, but I got a trick or two left in me still."

Yellow's fingers paw at the shotgun shell jar as effective as a declawed cat working the arm of your favourite leather chair.

Gravity stomps her leaded foot and that old rocking chair shoots out like a curling rock — Hurry! Hurry hard!

Now you might think Yellow would land in a bawling, skin-wrapped heap of four-year-old, positively charged neutronium.

You might think that.

But no.

Yellow hits the ground feet first, smiles up his cocky little Johnny Twelvegauge smile and saunters off, thumbs hooked into his Pull-Ups®.

Physics has no lessons for Yellow.

Gravity fails to make her point.

That 120-year-old rocking chair says, "Wheee! Do it again! Do it again!"

Well, she ain't dead yet, i'nit?

Anyways, that smile melts Sis's mad like ice cubes in a bonfire. You can't stay mad at the boy. No one can. That boy, Yellow, a good boy really, sure got charm to match his energy. Too bad, Sis thinks, too bad he can't use that energy of his to do good.

Then she puts a hand to her mouth, thinks: Damn and double-damn. I'm s'posed to teach him how to harness that power for good. I'm a lousy mother. Too tired to cry and too tired to dam the flood of self-loathing rushing her way, Sis blurts a tear that stinks of lake-bottom water.

Chuckie puts a beefy paw between her shoulder blades — according to Chuckie, that's a hug — and says, "Listen, Sis. Leave him here with me. I'll take him fishing or something."

"Don't you dare take him down to River."

"As if. I know better than that."

He laughs.

Sis doesn't. Sis needs a sweat bath, a smudge, and a tea.

But not another whisktea. Like Sis said, one's enough.

Sis grabs Yellow. She plants kisses where his face was. Yellow, a hooked worm of a boy, squirms and fusses. Instead of kissing his mother, not even a polite little cheek kiss, a loud ugly one, I guess.

Chuckie laughs.

You might laugh when I tell you that little shit Yellow presses his lips to his mom's, like a sweet little kiss. All lovey and sweet. Then that little shit blows a giant raspberry.

Right into his mom's mouth.

A sloppy splatter of four-year-old spittle and neutronic germs.

She unhugs Yellow and jumps backwards like that raspberry of his fired from a 12-gauge.

Sis says, "Sick!"

Yellow laughs. Gotcha, Mommy, he thinks.

Shoulda seen that coming, Sis thinks. She wipes her mouth

and chin with her sleeve. You almost never see her do stuff as rude as that. Almost never.

Chuckie, slow-shaking his head, laughs. Chuckie thinks, kid needs some new material. His schtick's in a rut. But with his trademark grin, Chuckie says, "Better hurry up and get gone. I could change my mind."

Sis looks between her son and her brother and sees her sweat bath.

Out the door she dashes.

In dashes Young Purple. Purp for short. Young Purple, a yellow lab with maybe nine undamaged brain cells — probably born that way, it happens sometimes — likes food more than fetch, more than a good swim, but not more than a belly or back scritch. You know that spot, that one right at the base of the tail. Purp never tires of that.

He'll let you scritch him there all damned day long. Your fingernails will fill with dog dander and what all else. Your hand will stink like unwashed rug. Your hand will stink for days maybe, no matter how hard you scrub it. Purp's superpower almost beats out spəpəplánt's.

Almost, but not quite.

And Purp, he doesn't care. Maybe he likes you more now that you stink like someone he knows pretty well. You could be his sibling. Purp always wanted a big family, but Chuckie and Edna snipped that dream early on.

Edna says all men's brains live in their nut sack.

She says, "Purp left his brains in a tin dish on a steel tray at the vet's."

Chuckie says, "So?"

Edna says, "So you think that's what happened to you, hun?"

"Naaaaaaaah," he goes. "Nah, just fell on my head a coupla times."

They laugh. They know Chuckie never fell on his head. They know he is pretty bright.

Usually.

What's worse: a big-brained dog making 100,000 puppies, or a loveable idiot who doesn't even hump your guests' legs?

I don't have the answer. But any mutt that doesn't hump your leg, snipped or unsnipped, already has my vote.

You tell me.

And don't you think for one second that Edna thinks Chuckie will hump their guests' legs.

And don't you worry that maybe Chuckie will hump your leg if you visit him and Edna. Cos Edna put him on a short leash.

A very short leash.

Now I'm joking.

If Chuckie humped legs, he'd only hump Edna's. Chuckie hasn't humped Edna's leg since that one time, when they were sixteen. They'd had a few. And Chuckie didn't know better.

So, back to our story.

Think of Sis in her sweat bath singing songs as she pours water on the grandfathers. She softens like steamed willow boughs. So relaxed you could weave her into a basket. But don't. Hard to play mom when you're bound to a bunch of cedar bark, i'nit?

Now over at Chuckie's, Yellow has hold of Young Purple's tail.

"Giddy-yup go, you ornery old varmint! Giddy-yup go, or it's the glue factory for you!"

Purp sits, scratches behind his ear. He doesn't mind that little two-legged hanging off his tail, but wishes he would do what the Creator put him on the planet for: "Scritch my backside, loud two-legged!"

No one in Yellow's world says things like *giddy-yup* or *ornery old varmint,* or *it's the glue factory for you!* He learns such language from the TV. Those movies he watches with his great-grandfather teach him that language. John Wayne. Randolph Scott. Gary Cooper. Burt Lancaster. Henry Fonda. Kirk Douglas.

Mostly John Wayne and Randolph Scott.

And of course that famous Indian actor, the Rifleman. Like I said earlier, just try telling Yellow otherwise.

Purp, maybe smart enough to know his little two-legged will not scritch and scratch his itchy spots, so he sighs like an old mutt and plops onto the dusty grass, got that just-lost-my-marrow-bone-blues look on him. That one he gets when the bone rolls off the deck and don't roll back to his slobbery mouth.

Best not ask how Chuckie knows that look.

Chuckie gets a big idea. He winks at Purp. "Keep Nephew busy a minute, Purp."

Lolling-tongued Purp sighs as Chuckie sneaks from the room. The tall two-legged did not say, "treat"; he did not say, "dinner"; he did not say anything worth hearing. He thought about gnawing that deer's tibia. Maybe it has more marrow to suck.

He thought about them scritches the high-voiced two-legged gave when she had them long red nails.

In walks Chuckie. "Hey, Nephew. Leave Young Purple alone for a second. Turn on the tube, hey? Let's see if them cartoons is on."

"Scooby Dooby Dooby Doo, where are you?"

Yellow chants "Scooby" all the way to the old TV. Scooby. Scooby. Scooby.

He pushes the on button. Scooby. Scooby. Scooby.

He pulls the on button. Scooby. Scooby. Scooby.

"Uncle! You tricking me?"

Scooby. Scooby. Scooby. He creeps behind the TV. Scooby. Scooby. Scooby. He traces the cord to the wall. Scooby. Scooby. Scooby.

Chuckie, lower lip extended, nods. That boy, he thinks. Pretty smart, that boy.

"Look around, Neph. The power musta went out."

Yellow's whole body collapses into a pout. His face screws itself into a spongeful of tears.

Chuckie says, "You know how we can fix it?"

Yellow knows. You get out the coal oil lamps, the candles, the wooden matches from way up high on the big-people-only shelf, and you curse out the hydro people until them lights come back on. But there's no way his uncle will make him say swears ever again. No goddamned way.

Oops.

Now's as good a time as any to tell you that Chuckie has one cow left in his field. One he and Edna didn't have the heart to sell when they had to scale down their farm some years back.

They call her Fred, named after Edna's brother. Anyways, Fred's milk's dried up, so all she does is eat, fart, shit, and sleep.

Chuckie leads Yellow to Fred's field. Along the way he picks up a galvanised two-quart funnel. Fred's field has no gate. She has seen life on the outside and wants nothing to do with it.

Now Chuckie picks up an old whiskey bottle, a length of even older garden hose, and a roll of Duck Tape®.

He tapes one end of the hose to the funnel, and the other to the bottle.

"You see Fred there? Fred makes gas for the generator."

Fred gots no hose. Fred gots no numbers on her face. Fred gots them numbers hided in her mouth? That why you never open your mouth, Fred? Fred gots numbers insteada teethes. Numbers insteada teethes. I want numbers insteada teethes. Numbers. Teethes. Teethes. Numbers. She gots numbers insteada teethes? Do cows gots teethes? Never seed cow teethes.

Hey, wait a sec. Wait one sec. Somethin else not right here. Somethin else wrong. Fred don't got Esso® painted on her. Don't got Shell® painted on her. Don't got PetroCan® painted on her. Don't got Chevron® painted on her. So what kinda gas Fred got?

Better not be same kinda gas Uncle gots. Auntie says Uncle gas makes green grass brown, makes white walls yellow. Uncle gas make me cry. Not sad cry, but. Fred don't smell like Grampa's truck. The air around her smells of cow poopies, not gas.

Yellow asks, "How Fred?"

"Her farts got superpowers."

Sure they do. Fart gotsa cape? Fart gotsa mask? Fart. Fart. Far-ar-ar-art-farty-fart-fart.

"They do not," says Yellow. "Do not. Do not. . . . Do mine?"

"Naaaaaaaah! Not your puny-human farts."

"Mine not puny!" Yellow bends over and grunts. *Pllurp!*

He grunts a little harder. *Plllllllurp!*

He sucks in a giant breath and he pushes, and grunts long. Grunts and pushes harder than he ever pushed in any of his four years:

PLLLLLLLLLLLLLLLLLLLLLLLLLLLLLLLLLLLLLLLLLLL LLLLLLLLLLLLLLLLLLLLLLLLLLLLLLLLLLLLLLLLLURP!

Pee-u. Chuckie thinks, My nephew maybe blew an o-ring.

"See?"

Yellow, all red in the face, looks more his mom after she brung home that spelling test she got her first 100% and gold star on. Chuckie's laugh tears paint his face.

Then Yellow laughs, too. Because farts are fun-fun-funny. ʔÚu! Funny and warm.

When he can talk again, Chuckie says, "Hope them Pull-Ups® got windshield wipers."

"Why?"

"Cos I think you got a lotta spray with that one."

Yellow frowns. Spray? That means my gots superpower farts? Super Fart. (*titter*) Superfartfart. (*titter*) Suuuuuuuuuper fart. (*titter*)

Chuckie sniffs the air over Yellow. Sis would lift the kid up and sniff his butt. So would Edna. But not Chuckie. He would cut a hole in the outhouse big enough to stick his head out, if Edna would let him.

"You got crap in your drawers?"

Yellow shakes his head so hard it looks like an airplane propeller. A bright red airplane propeller.

"How bout we change it anyways? Look good for Super Fred, hey?"

Yellow staggers a bit. Maybe shook his head too hard. Chuckie puts the contraption down in Fred's line of sight. She lows and sidesteps away from it. Chuckie thinks, You remember, i'nit? Fred, lowing, nods her head.

Chuckie hefts Yellow up. Even at arms length, a huge stink slinks from the boy. He crosses his fingers, sucks in a giant breath. Be a nugget. Be a nugget. Be a nugget.

Eyes closed, Chuckie sticks a set of crossed fingers under the waistband and puuuuuuuuulls it.

One-eye-squinty peek.

Not.

Squint gets a little bigger.

A.

Squint the size of the moon.

Nugget.

Inside of Yellow's Pull-Ups® looks like a Jackson Pollock canvas.

Chuckie thinks, One good fart, that one. It will be a story he tells when Yellow brings girls home for dinner. It will start, "Then there's the time Yellow here thought his butt had super powers. Hey Neph, member that one? . . ."

Chuckie will stretch the story out long enough to make Yellow burn red from the tips of his toes to the tips of his hair. In the best part of the story, he will say he had to spray down

Yellow's backside with the garden hose, and Yellow howled and squealed and kicked and fussed so much that he got his own poop in his hair, and had to shower under the kitchen faucet, and Chuckie had to wash him down with dish soap. And cos Yellow quacks and squirms and flails around.

He oopses way too much dish soap onto his nephew.

Rinse.

Rinse.

Rinse.

Chuckie will tell Yellow's girlfriend, "That boyfriend of yours screamed so much, you'd think I was waterboarding him." That story will help make his nephew a man, a good man. Maybe. But till then, Chuckie wrangles Yellow into new Pull-Ups® and thinks to tell Edna, when we decided not to make babies, we got it right.

So Chuckie thinks a little about Fred the sky-cow's story and says, "I dunno. Maybe cos she come down from the sky. Yeah. Down she came with a whomp that rattled your great-grandpa's uppers. Shook the tea from his mug.

"Yup, down she come, made a crater that took out most of the orchard."

"Nooooooo! Mom says Fire took it."

"Your mom's smart, but she don't always remember things right. Now do you want that story or what?"

Yellow nods an exuberant *yes*. That's fancy talk for *crazy-happy*.

"So, your great-grandpa and great-gramma run out to see what's the what. And you know what the what is, i'nit?"

"Freddie! Fred! Fred!" says Yellow. "Suuuuuuuuuuuuper Freeeeeed!"

Fred munches a mouthful of straw. Them two-leggeds' blah-blah-blahs give her gas. Her tail swish-swishes back and forth, forth and back, swatting away their deer-fly words. Go away, let me eat.

Fred farts.

Yellow laughs, cos, well, fart.

Chuckie laughs, cos. Well. Fart.

"Yeppers."

Fred lifts her tail. Fred shows Yellow exactly why you don't let a cow live in your house, and why the only cow you bring into the kitchen has visited a butcher first. Fred pivots till her backside faces away from them. For good measure she sidesteps three steps.

"Anyways, your great-grandparents walk into that smoking hole and find Fred chewing her cud. Her fur's a little singed is all. Looks up at them with those same big brown eyes gawking our way now."

"Like Superman?" says Yellow.

She side-eyes Chuckie's contraption, too, cos when them really old two-leggeds shuffled Fred's territory, they tried filling her up with jizz from Tony Anthony's prize bull, Barney, after Barney showed no interest in Fred, and Fred even less interest in Barney. Sky-cow Fred and prize-bull Barney had no idea what perfect calves they could have made.

No idea at all.

Nothing as fancy as a vet with a fistful of frozen Barney-jizz, not even a turkey baster, just that two-quart galvanised funnel and a clear plastic lunch bag full of a fresh load from that bull. Fred fears nothing except that funnel. Don't you worry, I never tell that story.

At four years old, Yellow knows more about the comic books and cartoon TV than he does about his own family. And his mother doesn't even own a TV set.

"Yeah, kinda like Supe, for sure, hey? But a cow."

"You tricking me, Uncle?"

"Naaaaaaaah! And she only has one superpower."

"Her farts make generator gas, i'nit?"

"Yeppers."

"How?"

"Fred won't say."

"She's a cow. Cows don't talk!"

"Sure they do! Anyways, she's a supercow."

Yellow wiggles his arse end while chicken-stepping small circles. He sings, "Butt. Butt. Supercow butt-butt."

"Listen, Nephew. I need you to do a real important job."

Yellow stands stone still. Yellow lives for important jobs. Somehow, this important job will fix the broken electricity. Will this one also make him Supercow's Jimmy Olsen?

Or maybe even better, Batcow's Robin! Na-na-na-na-na-na-na-na, Batcow! Pow! Whizz! Pop! Bam!

Na-na-na-na-na-na-na-na, Batcow!

"Hey nephew, you get all that?"

"Na-na-na-na-na-na-na-na." Yellow shakes Supercow, na-na-na-na-na-na-na-na, Batcow, and all the super villains from his head. He counts them as they hit the ground at his feet: one, two, four, two, six, three, four, seven . . . His head now empty, Yellow could listen.

Chuckie continues, ". . . it takes about three good farts to fill this bottle."

Yellow na-na-na-na-na-na-na-nods.

He screeches, "Wait! Wait just one god —"

Na-na-na-na-na-na-na-na, oops. "Wait a sec, Uncle."

"What?"

"You tricking me?"

"Naaaaaaaah! Why would I try to trick you?"

"Cos you always do."

"Then what bug's crawled up your butt?"

"Bugs? What if Supercow Super Fred poops on me?"

"He he he. Jump outta the way, unless you like cow-poop baths."

"Sick!"

Now you're about to see why I told that little story about Barney, the two-quart funnel, and Fred. Fred, who has as much superpower as you, circles her back-end away from the little two-legged and the infernal contraption. As uncomfortable as the cold skinny bits of the funnel felt, it didn't hurt her a bit. She simply objected to anyone violating her, no matter how soothing the old two-legged cow's songs and warm hands rubbing her neck, ears, and throat soothed.

"Supercow! Na-na-na-na-na-na-na-na, Batcow! Supercow, stop!" Yellow chants and chicken steps dodging and weaving away from Fred's swishing tail.

Chuckie points his lower lip at Fred's behind. "Good work,

Nephew. You almost gotter. Remember, you'll get your prey as long as you go slow and patient."

"Slow and patient, Supercow. Slow and patient, Batcow. I will get your magic farts and watch Scooby Dooby Dooby Doo."

"I'ma build a fire. Make fresh tea. You need anything, you holler. Got it?"

Yellow sings and chicken steps toward Fred's back end. Fred pivots her behind away from the boy, side-eying that annoying little two-legged and that infernal contraption.

Chuckie flicks on the main breaker, plugs in the electric kettle. He enjoys a smoke and a green tea on the back porch.

Yellow creeps toward Fred's backend. Na-na-na-na-na-na-na-na, Batcow! The contraption bomp-bomps behind him. Na-na-na-na-na-na-na-na, Batcow!

As she sidesteps away from Yellow's grabby little hands and behind him, the bomb-bomping contraption, Fred flicks her tail at the little-two-legged. No-no-no-no-no-no-no-no, Naughty Boy!

If necessary, Fred can shuffle around her pen all day and all night. In her head she hums "Puttin' on the ritz." Silly two-leggeds wearing crackers instead of eating them RITZ® crackers.

Silly cow doesn't know that *ritz* and RITZ® two different words. Silly language, that English.

To keep from tiring of the annoying little two-legged and his infernal contraption, Fred shuffles across her yard, stink-eyes the tea-sipping chain-smoking old two-legged, and lows at the fence until the little one catches up to her. Then she side-steps him, humming "Puttin' on the ritz," and wishing that annoying little two-legged would go ahead and stick that cuss-ed contraption up his own pee hole.

Hours pass and Yellow is no closer to catching Fred's farts. The contraption drags behind him, bomp-bomping over patches of crab grass. Bomp-bomp-tunking over plop-splattered rocks. The funnel's lip is dented and caked with dung. The Duck Tape® holding the funnel to the hose has shredded, leaving only five or ten threads stuck to the funnel. The bottle holds fast.

And Chuckie smokes and sips tea.

Yellow, on a mission, carries on, despite the fact his hands cramp, his feet burn, and he wants to sleep.

And Yellow never wants to sleep.

Chuckie picks up his nephew. "Good work out here. Good job."

"But Scooby . . ." murmurs Yellow.

"Lookit! You did it. You got the power back up."

Chuckie pats Fred's bony back end. He boots the contraption toward the edge of Fred's pasture.

Fred munches her cud. Good, them crazy two-leggeds finally got something better to do.

Yellow falls asleep on the couch. Scooby and the gang prattle on in the background.

Sis shows up around nine. She has that just-got-laid look to her. Relaxed as her sleeping son.

She expects Yellow to run straight into her arms, crying Mom-mom-momeeeeeeeeeeeeeeeee!

Sis thinks, Being a mom's a pretty good gig, i'nit?

The house stands still. Sis says, Too quiet.

The quiet shakes that beautiful calm, but doesn't break it.

Chuckie's better with kids than most fathers Sis knows. Happy and sad, that, thinks Sis. Sad and happy.

She walks around back, sneaks in through the kitchen. She expects Chuckie to meet her at the door. He always does. You just can't sneak up on that guy.

Go ahead. Try it.

The door clicks closed behind her.

No Chuckie.

She peeks into the other room.

Peaceful in the blue glow radiating from the TV set, her slack-jawed boy snores on the couch. She settles into the 120-year-old rocker, wraps Edna's woollen shawl around her and falls asleep smiling at her son and brother.

She could ask Chuckie for his secret. He might tell her a story. He might tell her a whopper. He might tell her the truth hidden in whopper-like words.

Best not to ask, i'nit?

You know I could tell her his secret, but like Chuckie, my lips stay sealed.

Next morning, all jungle-mouthed and slept-in clothes, Sis makes bannock and scrambled eggs. Sis's bannock, although not as good as Edna's — who's is? — makes your mouth water. Makes you eat one piece more than you should. Well the bannock itself doesn't make you do anything. You just blame it.

It's easier that way.

Yellow can't care less about whose bannock tastes better. Pour Lumberjack Syrup® on it, and it's the best bannock he's

ever had. *The best!* A year from now he will fall in love with his
Auntie Edna's bannock, topped with Imperial® margarine —
cos he wants that crown to appear on his head and he will sing,
dah dah-dah-daaaaah! Then check his head for the crown.
With or without the crown, Auntie Edna's bannock is *the bestest
of the best.*

Not even grudgingly, Sis will agree. Sis sometimes puts in
cinnamon, sometimes sliced banana, sometimes blueberries.
Even so, Yellow still says his Auntie's bannock is *the bestest of
the best.*

Kids. Right?

Back to breakfast now.

Chuckie splits his bannock in half. Inhales the steam. Shovels
his scrambled eggs between the two halves. No margarine.
No bacon. No sausage. Just bannock and scrambled eggs.

"What'd you two do yesterday? Did you go fishing?" Sis asks.

I'm pretty sure she knows they didn't go fishing. Chuckie
probably said they would to tease her. Cos Sis fears Yellow will
run off and get swallowed up by River. Take her son the same
way She took his father.

Yellow sings, "I caught farts for the generator."

Yellow laughs. He can say *fart* at the dinner table and not
get swatted upside the head.

"You what?" says Sis.

"Supercow Fred. Na-na-na-na-na-na-na-na Batcow Fred,
ma-ma-ma-ma-ma-ma-ma Mom." He threshes another chunk
of bannock. "You know her farts are the gas that keep the
generator running."

Through gritted teeth and poison-glare eyes, Sis says, "Super-cow? Batcow? Magic farts?"

Chuckie points at his masticating jaw. He fakes a food orgasm and slows down his chewing and thinks: food tastes better when you chew it real slow.

He stops chewing, swishing it into a bannock and scrambled egg slurry he swallows bit by bit.

"Good bread, Sis. Tastes a lot like Mom's."

Sis nods.

Inside her pride fires up its marching band and throws itself a ticker-tape parade.

"So, cow farts?"

"You remember when we was kids? Dad usta send us out to catch Fred's super farts?"

"Yeah, Mom! Gramps always sent you to get gas for the generator, i'nit, Uncle?"

"And you know how much she hates that funnel?"

"Riiiiiiiiiiiiiiight."

She now knows how they spent their day. Her brother's even smarter than she thought.

"I couldn't get her to fart in that bottle. But she farted so much the generator worked all by itself."

"Damn power went out again."

Yellow pouts, "Right when Scooby Dooby Dooby Doo was starting."

Sis thinks, Smart guy, my brother. She smiles. "Guess I forgot."

Yellow lifts a cheek and cuts a loud fart. He sings, "Super farts."

Chuckie and Sis say, "What'd I tell you about farting at the dinner table?"

"It was on accident."

Sis says, "Accident my eye."

"Better check your pants, Nephew. I think you crapped in 'em again."

Sis says, "Again?"

Chuckie winks at Yellow. "No bigs, Sis. Hey, Nephew?"

Now Yellow doesn't know the word *conspiracy,* but he knows what one is. Fooling Ma-mama-ma-ma-ma-ma-mommy.

So, that's the story of how Yellow spent a day catching farts with Fred and Uncle Chuckie.

Snḱyép and His
Shiny New Choker

This one day that tricky Coyote says, "Time for me to get out and see what's the what."

So out he goes, singing a song about blue skies, and that song so pretty. So pretty them birds stop doing what they do, and them birds sing along. You got them crows, them ravens, and even that Magpie, singing harmony like only them birds can sing, and all them birds hop from pine tree to fir tree to pine tree. So many of them birds singing along that them trees sway, singing, "Shhh-shhh, shhh-shhh," like rattles, and become part of Coyote's blue sky song.

Them birds and them trees keep time with Coyote, singing their beautiful song about Sky so blue.

But Sky? Maybe she think it a sad song. Cos that Sky? She screw up her eyes.

And those eyes of hers? The colour of mid-May afternoon.

Them eyes cloud up and spit rain as heavy as hail on Coyote and his chorus of birds, so he bolt for cover, and them birds hop inside Cedar's tight-knit branches, mostly dry and safe, and they laugh at Coyote as he runs for cover.

And he get cover all right.

Inside a perfect, round cave in a nearby mountain.

Scratching his wet head, suspicious, and maybe confused, snk̇yép says, "A mountain? That one must be new. I never seen it before."

(Now you and I, we know that mountain's no mountain.

No, that mountain, just a pile of Big City garbage, a pile of Big City sewage, and Big City shit dumped on Coyote's land, out of sight of Big City people. But Coyote? I guess he don't know about Big City and Big City shit.)

Coyote says, "This one different from all the rest. Soft and mooshy, got a smell to it. Got a familiar smell to it, but not a smell from around here. And its rocks all pretty, smooth, and mostly shiny. Some of them as white as baby's teeth. Some of them as yellow as ripe corn. Some of them redder than a Great Lakes sunset. And not a single blade of grass. And not a single prickly pear. And not a single sage bush, well, no living sage, anyways. Except some caught head first around that new mountain's base.

(Yeah, just dead tumbleweeds, blown into that mountain of Big City shit.)

So Coyote, he dive over that ring of tumbleweed and into that perfect, round cave — (That cave? just an old washing machine.) — inside the perfect centre of that huge white rock, half-unveiled in that new mountainside. And that Sky's tears rain down, ting off Coyote's cave, like when it bounce off old Harvey Andrew's tin-roofed shed. Not unpleasant, that *ting ting ting ting*.

So Coyote curl up,

and slip his nose under his tail.

And that smell there kinda remind him of that mountain, the one holding that cave, this one, keeping him dry.

Sniffing his butt hole, Coyote murmur, "But that can't be. Cos I would know of any creature in my territory big enough to leave behind a pile like that."

Sky's rain song sing him into peaceful sleep.

That Coyote drop into sweet sleep, and dream of chasing his wife's sister again. And catching her again. And loving her up, in a good way. Again.

They love each other up, them two, snk̇y̓ép and his wife's sister. In a perfect, round cave whose walls sing back to them two. Coyote and his wife's sister, their song of lust, and pleasure.

Coyote jolt from his beautiful dream, shaken from sleep by a world-ending rumble. A monstrous hiss and roar. And the world around him, now cast into deep blackness. And now cast inside a silence he hasn't heard since that first time he awoke, and walked this world alone.

So Coyote think he can restart the world, and maybe do things different this time. Maybe better.

(Coyote must be addled from sleeping with his head too close to his butt, cos you and I, we know that Coyote can't create anything.)

So Coyote suck in a huge breath before he start tunnelling through this new mountain into a world he can remake.

He think about the sort of land he'll make this time. And think about the sort of two-leggeds he'll let in this time. And think about the sort of birds he'll let in this time: more crows and ravens and magpies for sure, cos together, we sing so good. O, wait, maybe not them birds.

Coyote stop his digging, says: "Hey, our song made Sky cry. And what if she cried so much the top of this big, soft mountain bleed onto me while I dream? What if . . . What if our song, that one we sang together, buried our old world. And left me alone to start all over again? Making a new world every time we gather and sing seem a lotta work. And some days I got better things to do. So maybe I won't make them birds after all. Maybe take away their voice. Maybe sour their sweet song."

So Coyote, almost out of breath, dig through shit and stuff, through slime and goo, and finally he break the surface. He wheeze in a huge breath, and see a world almost exactly like that old one.

Sky above, mottled grey and blue, and that Cedar, dripping rain, and full of his old buds. Them crows. Them ravens. And that Magpie, stunned silent as that Coyote shake off that Big City shit, Big City goo.

Coyote, all slick and greasy, says, "Behold! I dreamed a new mountain. And here it stands, right where I dreamed it."

Say them crows and them ravens: "Why you dream yourself underneath of it then? And moan for your sister-in-law, hey?"

Draped in his solemn suit, Magpie says: "No dream brought that new mountain. No. A monster like a giant snake, maybe, rumbled through here while you dreamt. And that monster slither through here. Leave a shit on your mountain cave. That huge shit on it, that mountainous turd you just swam through."

"No," protests fast-thinking Coyote. "No. That cannot be, for I dreamt this mountain. I did. And I awoke to find it here."

(In it, more like.)

Well, that Magpie, he shed his solemn suit. He shed that suit and laugh. (Wouldn't you laugh at such a silly lie?)

Them crows and them ravens? Them birds croon, "ʔÚu, skéw, x̣ə́xt skéw. ʔúu, x̣ə́xt skéw!"

Coyote, he sniffs, says, "Fine. Don't believe me."

Magpie says, "It's you not believing me. But go. Follow that trail there. That one there. In front of you."

"This one," asks skeptical snkẏép. "This funny looking snake trail?"

"Yeah, yeah, that the one," say them crows and them ravens.

"You sure?"

Them ravens sigh. Them crows sigh. Together, them ravens and them crows say, "Why would we lie to you?"

Coyote think on this a minute. Then he think long and hard about him dressed in a long purple gown, trimmed with sable and white rabbit fur. With buckskin pockets. Them pockets got long, swaying fringes. He think to add silver conchos, but change his mind — Maybe them conchos just a little too much. Don't I look good and royal already? — Wearing a gold hat covered in polished stones from that monster shit. Then he forget all about them royal clothes. Think some more about the monster and his giant shit.

Finally, chest all puffed out, Coyote says, "Maybe. Just maybe something to what you say, Magpie. Maybe a monster after all. I'll show him. You watch. You'll see."

And them birds? Them crows, them ravens, and that Magpie, they paint on their gravest faces. They make them most serious eyes. But their laughing ones crack that serious paint.

Coyote slip on that new mountainside, that mountain of Big City shit. He slip and stumble down. Down. Down. Jet a wake of bad-smelling stuff.

"You gonna track that beast?" ask Magpie. Snk̇ẏép, he nod. "Then maybe you should roll around in that mess some more, hey? Go deep undercover. Fool that monster so good, maybe make it think you come from its own butt?"

"Hey," says Coyote, "good thinking there."

So Coyote drop and roll around. Coat himself good and thick. Got small stones and pebbles. Them rocks, real light. Real colourful, too. All green, blue, yellow, and red. Some of them rocks dangle from the tips of his fur. Tangled in his fur, his tail. He snip at his tail, thinking maybe it someone else's.

"Behave like you look," says Magpie. "Look at you, all dressed up like you a warrior ready to scrap."

Now that Coyote, he beam like a new dad. His smile so big, his mouth fall off from the weight of it. And it sink into the muck. And that muck seep inside. Its stink stick to the tongue, the teeth, and the roof. That mouth cough and gag and spit and cough.

"Hey!" shout that mouth. "Hey, get me outta here!"

So that Coyote put his mouth back in his face. He spit.
He gag. He cough. He wipe off that muck on the back of a paw,
then spit and gag some more.

"Now look at you," preens Magpie. "Look at you, teeth like
a movie star. Regalia like the finest pow wow dancer. But you
missing something, i'nit? You need one more thing. Just one
more piece to show that monster you a great warrior. A great
chief, and not someone to mess with. Hmm, I see that one thing
just a few feet from this old cedar."

Coyote sees nothing, but them smooth, shiny rocks: silver,
gold, copper, green, nine different shades of blue, even a pink
one, or two.

Coyote think, What a guy gotta eat to make his shit so pretty?

"I don't see nothing," says Coyote. "I don't see nothing at all."

Magpie point to a shiny silver rock and says, "Look there."

"Here?" asks Coyote.

He pick up that silver rock, all hollow and coppery on the
inside. Hollow and smooth as River's rocks. Got a piece of green
paper stuck to it.

"This the piece I need?" asks Coyote.

"Yeah-yeah, yeah-yeah," says Magpie. "That it all right."

Coyote scrunch up his nose, twist his face into a scowl, and
he says, "Hey, look! A name tag stuck to it. Name of Del Monte
Tomatoes #10. You think Del Monte Tomatoes #10 gonna miss it?"

"No-no, no-no," says Magpie. "Old Del got at least nine more.
He won't miss that one. So just yank off that name tag."

Them crows and them ravens, hold their breath. And wait.

"That rock," says Magpie, "maybe make a fine choker. And make you a noble warrior. A formidable warrior. A fearsome hunter. Not a creature to mess with. You get that monster running scared, and he never shit in your woods again."

"Yeah-yeah," say them crows and them ravens. "Make him take his dump elsewhere."

Coyote's chest inflate like a blimp, and his smile start to weigh him down, cos it get so big. But Coyote clamp down on that smile. Stop it before it get too big again.

Coyote look at that stone Del Monte Tomatoes #10 lost. He says, "This look like the shed skin of a rock."

"Now it a choker," say them crows and them ravens.

"Of course," says Coyote. "I knew that."

As Coyote slip that old tomato can over his muzzle, he says (his voice, all cop yelling, "put your hands where I can see them"): "Hey, this stone smell like tomato and salt! Smell so good I could eat it up."

(That coyote's own voice curl his own tail up between his legs.)

The serious paint on them crows and them ravens melt off. That serious paint on Magpie? It melt, too. And they laugh tears. Coyote fold back his ears and push that stone over his head, tight around his neck, but not too tight.

"Look at you," says Magpie.

"Ow whoo," say them crows and them ravens.

"A braver warrior I never seen," says Magpie. "And that choker? Wearing your choker like that, no monster could bite your throat. No arrow could pierce it. No blade could slit it."

82

And Coyote, he tip his head at them ravens, them crows and that Magpie. He shake the muck off a piece of rebar. Heft it like a spear.

"Off to battle," says Coyote. "Off to war. No more monster shitting in my woods. No more monster shitting on my land."

This story ends here, with Coyote armed, and ready for war.

The One About the Boy
and the Grey Squirrel

this kid I knew got the blood thirst young
    wanted to hunt, he say'd, about five that first time
    shoulderin his father's thirty-aught-six
    like soldiers he'd seen on the boob tube, some show
    Rat Patrol maybe, I guess it don't matter much
    coulda been that *Gomer Pyle,* too
    kid lived in front a that thing
        that boob tube
yeah, I guess I say'd blood thirst
damn kid wanted to kill somethin
      not like he tortured the dog, or burned up ants
with wunna them magnifying glasses
      no, no, nothin like that
so just a kid who didn't know yet
    what it meant to hunt
        to take a life outta need

---

so this kid, marchin round the kitchen
    barely strong enough to hoist his dad's gun
    hoists it on his shoulder all army-guy like
        marchin round the kitchen table
    knocks over a cup, the salt and pepper shakers
        hurtin nothin, except the front sight
    dad, hoppin mad, snatches his gun from his son
        spends the next two hours tryin to get that sight right
            every time that gun miss a buck
             he reset that front sight
    resets it every time it miss a moose
        or that no trespassin sign old Cooter MacDonald hung
    ' on his fence
            out Potani, that sign facin the road?
             like Cooter owns that land he squats on
That Dad, instead a punishin
    his kid for playin with his gun
    he gets his kid a twenty-two calibre pellet gun
        a Crossman twenty-two break-barrel
            CO_2 cartridge powered, beaut of a gun
perfect for a kid, one old enough to break that barrel, hey?
    kid needed someone to load his gun
        needed to rest it on a fence rail, or something
but that kid? he sure could shoot
and one day, out with his father crashin through the bush
    after grouse
they stop to take a drink, must a bin one-ten in the shade
    at least one-ten, maybe one-fifteen

a heat so dry it shrivels the eyes
and them two, father and son,
they rest against a cottonwood
    in shade as hot as a bread oven
the water they brung rises like steam from a boiling kettle
    yeah, that hot, but still not the hottest day we ever had
        that one happened before my time
that day got so hot, they say'd, so hot River went down five feet
    dropped five whole feet between sunup and sunset
        that day, the hottest one ever, say'd the old timers,
           the ones that would know such things
so this day
the one that father and his boy out huntin grouse
them two sittin under a cottonwood
evaporatin like an inch of water on River's bed
father tellin the boy about his first time out huntin with
    his father
in winter, snow up to his eight-year-old arse
    huntin rabbit, maybe grouse, and his own father
hopin to bag a moose someone say'd they'd seen
but they seed no scat, nothin
    not a single sign a moose anywhere in them bushes
all the while he's tellin his tale
a grey squirrel chews them two out
that five-year-old boy and his dad
yeah, that dad goes,
I seen a hare, bout thirty yards up
nose twitchin, ready to bolt under a deadfall

first one we seen all day, that rabbit
    that hare
        and me, all tired from haulin this twenty-two
through thick bush, and snow up past my arse
    thinkin we grab this rabbit, this hare
        we could go home
            have some bannock and tea while we warm up
so I pull back the bolt
    slip a shell inside the chamber
        like I'd done at least two hundred times before
            flick off the safety
here, the kid's father stops his story
you hear nothin but River's faint roar
and sweat drippin off nearby trees
and that grey squirrel chitterin
    so worked up, its tail ties itself into a knot
so I pull my gun up, easy as aimin at tin cans
    sight that rabbit
        that hare
            sight a spot right between his eyes
and I take in a deep breath
    slowly let it out
        all this happenin in the space between two thoughts
just before the last of my air steams out my nose
    POP!
        that rabbit, that hare drops dead where he sat
so Dad, he takes my rifle
    he takes my rifle, then hands me his Bowie knife

and tells me how to dress out my hare
    walks me through it
        right there in that snow
anyways, we take my hare, that rabbit home
and Mom
she butchers it
chops it up, and throws it in a pot with some onions,
    some potatoes, some carrots
        and a can of tomato paste
            we got from the Chinaman's store
while me and Dad we sit near the wood stove
    sittin near the wood stove with tea, bannock and jam
        listenin to Hank Williams records
            tryin to get warm
and that squirrel,
that grey squirrel, louder still
pretty much shoutin over that father's rabbit huntin story
so that boy's father
he goes, *think you're ready to bag your first critter?*
    yeah, that boy answers, *and after*
    can I wear his tail on my belt?
that father, he laughs, and says, *sure but you got to get it, first*
he pops a pellet into his boy's gun
gets down on all fours
tells his son to rest the gun on his back
    reminds him not to hold his breath
        yeah, yeah, I know it, that boy says
and that squirrel, it chitters louder

almost sounds like it's callin out them two-legged
trespassers
so the boy sights that squirrel, and his dad
chest all puffed out, smirks
one side of his head ready to tell him, *better luck next time*
the other crowin to his buds about the squirrel his boy
just a boy, barely five, barely talkin and walkin
but a crack shot, just five and his boy bags a squirrel
who would a thought this kid, barely outta diapers
shootin somethin alive
for the first time in his life
could hit that squirrel square between its eyes?
for sure not me, maybe not even his own father
so when that squirrel squeals out in pain
shrieks and drops outta that tree
like a rock off a cliff it drops
and not a drop a blood anywhere
lands on its back
legs up
and spread like they still cling to a branch
little kid squeaks himself
more mouse than cougar now
he and his father gawk at that fallen squirrel
I guess that's when that little kid sees them teats
all pink and swollen and stretched, six a them
six teats, all fat with milk
and that little guy goes, *what's wrong with him, Dad?*

and that boy's father says, *he's a she and got*
some babies in a nest somewhere
maybe up that same tree
and that little boy bursts into tears
      he cries so hard that Sun can't melt them tears as fast
      as he makes them
he says, *sorry, I didn't know you'd die*
I don't want you to die
his father don't say nothin, except, *too late, she's already gone on*
and then he hands his boy a stick
tells him to dig a hole and put that squirrel in it
      that father never had a taste for squirrel
         can't say I know many who do
and that boy blubbers on his knees gettin
      nowhere with that squirrel's grave
so the father snatches up the stick and carves out a bitty grave
pulls his skinnin knife and asks, *you want that tail for your belt?*
that kid?
he shakes his head
like you just asked him if he wants a shit sandwich
so they bury that squirrel, cover up her grave with some rocks
and that boy?
he don't let his father talk about it all the way home
and some days later the boy goes
    so Dad?
so Dad, what you think happened to them baby squirrels?
his father thinks a minute

takes his sweet time

searchin for the right words, maybe
but that silence scares the boy anyways
I dunno, hope a raven got em
better than them starvin to death, hey?
yeah, just what that kid needed to know
so that boy?
he puts that gun, along with all the pellets
and that box a CO_2 cartridges
way in the back of his closet
underneath of old teddy bears
and other stuff he'd outgrew
and maybe that boy don't think about killin
and about shootin his gun for a good long time

and maybe one day he did

SPAM® Stew and the MALM Minimalist Bedroom Set from IKEA®

So this story tells about the time the old lady's sx̱ay̓wih came home for SPAM® stew, his favourite meal. Pretty good trick for a dead guy. You might not think a stew made of SPAM® worth pulling your dead bones from your grave, through town and up that mud-slick two-mile trail to the house, but you haven't tried the old lady's SPAM® stew.

The old lady never measured ingredients when she cooked.

"Ach! Maybe I could write it down. But I couldn't read it."

"But, Mum. I could read it. We don't want your recipes to die with you."

"Have I up and died on you?"

"You know what I mean."

Now the old lady chooses to drop the whole thing.

Her daughter Violet got back from treatment a week ago.

Violet stays with her mother. She doesn't leave the house for anything: "O, Mum. Cos everything's a trigger."

The old lady's question: "So whose finger's on it?"

Violet answers: "Everyone I ever known, Mum. You can't joke about stuff this serious." Before her mother can snark an answer, "But not you, Mum. Not you and Walter, for sure. You always watched out for me."

"Anyways, I told you a million times: you want to cook like me, work with me in my kitchen, and learn by watching and doing it."

So despite the triggers, or because of them, Violet will learn to cook with her mother. To can, and make pickles. To make wimmins bread, but not for a while, cos stringing them two words together gives her a minor breakdown. She cries for days, curled up in an unshowered fetal ball. She won't talk about it. Violet falls apart, but doesn't console herself with wine, or whiskey, or mouthwash, or vanilla extract. She doesn't crave it. Not even a beer, or ginger beer, or root beer. The old lady lets her alone. Under six wool blankets, Violet sweats, shivering like she has the TB, or pneumonia, or the DTS, or has withdrawal again. But no.

The old lady kisses the blanketed lump where Violet's pillow shows.

She knows that sometimes body memories – flashbacks – look like things they aren't. She won't talk about it, not in a way that makes sense to her own self. But she tells Violet – all of her kids, nieces and nephews – to sit with it till it can't sicken you the same way. She puts out hot tea for her three times a day, and she keeps fresh ice in the jug of water beside Violet's bed. Sometimes Violet drinks the chicken broth, despite its sickly yellow colour. Sometimes she sits beside Violet's bed, telling her stories, singing healing songs.

She kisses the blanketed lump where Violet's pillow shows.

She cackles the old woman cackle. "Better not be your ass I'm kissing, Daughter."

Then she rests a hand on the lump. "Sorry you got to go through this shit just to stay alive."

Taking care of fragile Violet's like annealing a knife blade, i'nit? Too much will ruin it, make it brittle and useless. Not enough and it won't work like it's supposed to.

She says, "Two more days of this. Two days and no more, then you go for a sweat bath. Steam with the grandfathers, not your own stink."

The lump of Violet under her blankets shakes and rattles like Regan MacNeil's bed. The old lady starts, "Ai-ee!"

Then that bed bucks like a frisky calf, wobbles off the floor, rising three feet, then five.

Lump of Violet stills.

Bed vibrates, bucks, and spins.

Violet, not so much a still lump now, whimpers like a roller-coaster-scared kid on El Toro. She hangs her head over the bed's raging edge, and vomits but not green-pea-soup-projectile vomit. But vomit is vomit. The old lady mops up the mess on the floor, sponge baths Violet, daubs her neck and forehead with cold cloths. Maybe two more days of this not enough, after all.

Gonna be a long, long night.

Another long night, the next one. Bed bucks and spins. Violet vomits, whimpers, and cries. The old lady mops up the mess.

Next morning, after taking green tea with lemon, they sit on the porch and watch the melons and peas grow.

Five days and nights the same. The old lady catnaps while beading or crocheting. Violet stares at the old water stain on her bedroom wall so long it performs a healing dance. Each time that stain's fan goes up a bit of happy air tingles away some of the ugly shivers Violet shoots out.

Fifth night as ugly as the last four.

Sixth dawn and Violet sips nettle tea, nibbles on toast with sour cherry jam, and picks at two eggs, scrambled. Bacon would've been nice, too, but the old lady says Violet's guts can't handle it now.

When they finish tea, the old lady washes Violet's hair, draws her an Epsom salt bath, and cleans her like a newborn. She sings prayers so low, like whispering to xeʔɬkʷúpiʔ.

Then she puts Violet to work in the garden. All morning pulling weeds, feeding, watering, pinching back oregano, basil, and dill.

The old lady uses her good shears to trim greens off some scallions. "You know what today is?"

Violet counts days on her fingertips. The arithmetic would be easier if she had a start date. "I dunno. The ninth?"

The old lady laughs. "It's your dad's birthday."

They laugh. Violet shakes her head: "The ninth. Sheeeee-it."

Violet now knows what date and what month, but not what day. But no job waiting, so the day doesn't matter. (It's Thursday.)

Heavy wheels flick rocks like bottle caps off the undercarriage of a truck down the road a ways. Dust hangs in the air like a wind-borne feather.

Violet perks up. "Sounds like Walter."

The old lady nods. "Could be. He said he might stop by today."

The old lady knows Walter's on the way home, for his father's birthday and he has a huge surprise for his baby sister.

Yeah, Walter drove all the way to Big Town to get that MALM minimalist bedroom set from IKEA®. (Maybe the only two things Walter hates: Big Town and IKEA®. Now those are two stories I might tell one day, but not now.) He gets lost. Drives by the airport three times. The fancy-schmancy GPS they put in his shiny new truck knows the city as good as Walter. Good thing his cousin Mildred gives good directions. One phone call to her, and Walter finds his way again.

Sure enough, some minutes later Walter backs his truck up close to the front door.

Violet steals a peek under the tarp. "You moving back home, qéck?"

"Something like that."

The old lady swats Violet's hand. "Get your nose out of your brother's business."

The three of them sip tea and eat baked bannock. They only eat it baked cos the old lady's blood is mostly lard. She has to eat it dry. Can't even sweeten it up with a little sour cherry jam. Violet learnt to make it in rehab. They printed recipes on little cards, three a week for all but the first week. (She cooks good when she has a written recipe to follow. But who doesn't, hey?) Therapy they called it. Violet and the women called it indentured labour, even them who wanted to cook for a living after they got all cleaned up.

The old lady gently pats the gooseflesh bubblewrapping her forearm. She sighs, half-smiling. Blows a little kiss at the ceiling.

So they sip tea and talk, the three of them. Four if you count the old man hovering above the kitchen table. So stealthy that old man, he sneaked away from his shadow. And that shadow stand in a field of bitterroot. And it passes for a gnarled old apple tree. But not so stealthy that he could sneak up on the old lady.

The old lady wombles off into the bush with a hatchet and machete so sharp that cedar boughs fall to the ground when she nears a tree.

Violet and Walter dig a fire pit about two feet deep and five feet in diameter. Another foot deeper and they could roast a hind quarter of moose in it. If they had one. But the fire will wipe the spirit haunting Violet's bed away and out of her life. Maybe for good.

They smudge, the three of them. The old man hovers above them, inhaling that sweet smoke. He envelopes himself in it. He smells the memory of it. He bathes in the memory of it.

Violet chops kindling. Walter chops seasoned pine and spruce. Nice logs they dragged from the bush two, maybe three years ago. On a bet, Walter whacked out a cord of it one-handed. On another bet, he whacked one out left-handed.

Yeah, that one hurt. Walter's a lot like that Chuckie when it comes to wagers. Neither of them two loses a bet. But people keep trying, like a stubborn slot machine, they expect it to pay out big-time one day.

So Violet stacks kindling, wads up pages from the Sears and Eaton's catalogues, then stuffs it into the stack of kindling.

Walter laughs, and pokes his sister in the ribs. "Look atchoo. Away for a coupla years, and forgot how to make a real fire."

"Ah, you. I could do it easy. I just love the colours them catalogue papers make when they burn."

"Yeah, sure. You just keep telling yourself that."

Pretty quick, that fire crackles and pops to life. Flames tinted with colours you don't see in nature. Pop and crackle like the old man pushing himself out of his chair at bedtime. But he doesn't pop and crackle any more. Just one bonus of death, I guess.

Two at a time, Walter hands Violet chunks of wood. Two at a time, she places it over and around the kindling.

Pretty quick that fire flare, too hot to throw smoke.

The old lady hands Violet a cedar bough.

Violet places it on the fire. It fwoooms fire, crackles and spits fiery embryos into the smoke plume it spews.

The old lady, two-stepping around the fire, sings healing prayers.

The old man two-steps alongside her, singing healing prayers.

The old lady doesn't think it strange that gooseflesh pop like burning spruce and pine.

Walter helps Violet haul everything from her bedroom. Everything except the plywood floor, ceiling, and walls.

Dresser. Dresser drawers. Dresser and drawers burn unearthly colours. Bed frame. Bed rails. Bed burns in unearthly colours. Night stand. Night stand drawer burn unearthly colours. Box spring throws black smoke. Mattress pukes black smoke. Sheets. Black smoke. Blankets. Black smoke. Pillow. Black smoke. Pillow case. Black smoke.

Black smoke shrieks pain.

One piece at a time, they put it on the fire. And after every piece bubble, shrivel, or snap in the flames and smoke, either black or unearthly, the old lady shakes a handful of sage mixed with juniper berries onto it.

So that fire burns good and long. Violet watches that fire, poking it with a stick, tossing pine and spruce into it. That fire has to burn to ash, and the ash has to burn to dust, and the dust has to stay buried.

Violet concentrates. She looks at how her life will unfold from this day onward. She sees good stuff in it, like a job with the band, as its D & A counsellor. Her three-year cake is a confetti angel cake. She graduates with a degree in Social Work four years after that. If the band funds her.

No.

They will.

The band will fund her.

They will.

Violet, all covered in soot, smoke, and dirt sweats beside the fire, feeding it all night long. Her father squats beside her, wafting in and out of visibility in the white smoke drifting on the rise and fall of Wind's lazy lungs. He spins stories of his brother as a boy, how he's not the same since falling from that apple tree. Lands on his head. Not the same since. Not always wrong in the head.

He don't come around no more.

He don't drink no more. Keeps pretty much to himself, living in a shack way out on Crown land. Couple times a year a nephew takes out a sack of flour, tins of coffee and tobacco, a box of tea, and a pail of lard. Brings back a stack of hides and pelts. Sells it all.

Puts enough cash aside to get next season's supplies. Puts the rest away for the girl's schooling. She needs a lotta snúye for D'n'A school, i'nit? And enough in them savings to pay for a coupla years of college now. Maybe four, if she lives cheap. Maybe gets some from the band. Maybe a little more from INAC. Naaaaaaaah, like that would ever happen. But who knows, hey?

You could blame his broken head. You could blame his drinking. He does still. So I guess he gotta stay in the bush till he sees it different. Like you, i'nit? He's my brother. And he made his choices and he's paying their price, i'nit? But you're my daughter. My baby. You could have a good life still. You will. Glad to see you leave the bush, my baby. An old man couldn't ask for a better birthday present. You gived it to yourself. Good. I'm sorry I failed you, my girl. I am.

Violet jolts alert. Three a.m. crickets sing like old-man laughter. She tosses two more logs onto the fire. Her old man drapes an arm around Violet.

She shivers in the three a.m. cold.

Walter builds a fire near the tall yellow cedar the old lady uses for her sweat baths. Soon the fire burns brighter than sunrise. He shovels in the grandfathers and sings under his breath.

Violet's seventh day starts with sunrise. Her eyes burn red. Her hands cramp like the old lady's. Her back aches. Her ass as numb as when she gets so lost in a book that she forgets she's sitting on the shitter. Not too different from walking out of a blackout drunk, just a few steps short of oblivion, back into that foggy reality you spent the last six days trying to escape.

The old lady helps Violet to her feet. Guides her to the sweat bath.

"Can I change outta these clothes first?"

The old lady purses her lips. "No. Start your bath with it on. Maybe take it off before the third round."

Violet laughs. "What makes you think I'll last three rounds, Mum?"

"I'll bring you clean ones to put on?"

And Walter says, "You better. Last thing I need to see's you running bare-arsed across the yard."

"Ha. Qéck, you think you're funny."

"Naaaaaaaah. I know it."

After her sweat bath, Violet paints her bedroom ceiling cerulean, and its walls dusty rose. She and Walter fit the floor with pink granite lino.

The old lady nods in the doorway. "Hang some pretty curtains, and I'll have to charge you twenty-five bucks a night to sleep over, i'nit!"

For nearly a whole breath, Violet takes the old lady serious.

Windows and doors open. *Ellen* blasting from the TV the old lady protested having in her home. She hasn't turned it off since Walter screwed it onto the wall. He and Violet got her a clicker that listens, and automatically switches to *Moosemeat & Marmalade,* and *North of Sixty,* whenever it's on.

"That TV's not so smart. I say find me something good to watch. It don't do nothing. Or it tells me it can't find it."

"Maybe it's smarter than you give it credit for, hey? Never anything good on it. 'Swhy they call it the boobtube."

"Thought they called it that for all the smut it plays after midnight."

While the paint dries and the glue under the lino hardens, Violet and Walter build the IKEA® MALM minimalist bedroom set. Walter bets they will have three bits left after they're done. Violet bets one. The old lady says none will be left, and she backs up her word by tossing a dollar onto the fancy-schmancy saucer Walter brought back from Victoria. It came with a cup. Turns out the saucer could fly — once — but the cup could not. Violet put in a buck. Walter put in a buck. A pool is not a wager, or Walter would have raised them twenty, to make it interesting. Both wish they had whiskey in their teacups. Both think it would be faster to make and season boards and then build furniture from it.

No extra parts this time.

Nearly dark by the time they get it done and slid into place. Curtains from that Sahali Superstore. Bedding from that Sahali Superstore. Too many ghosts in used bedding, used curtains.

Sometimes got to wash it five times to get them ghosts and old smells out of it, too. And really not too much cheaper than new from that Superstore. Harvesting other people's junk not quite the same as picking berries, ċewete?, or tetúwṅ. But finding a good used one sometimes more fun. Sometimes.

Sun's moved behind Mount Shasta, taking ten degrees of warmth with it.

"Hey, Mum, when's supper?"

"When you make it."

"When I make it? Holy! We don't even have enough bread for sandwiches."

"C'mon. Wash up and I'll show you how to make spam® stew and bannock."

"I already know how to make bannock."

"Mine?"

"Well, I would if you wrote it down."

The old lady shook her head. "Yeesh."

Walter finds a ball game, says over his shoulder: "Play nice, you two."

The old lady, her arms crossed, stands behind Violet. "Open two cans of spam® and pour it onto the cutting board."

She slides the eight-inch French knife from the blade block. "Now chop it into squares about this big."

"You mean like one-inch cubes, Mum?"

"'Swhat I said, i'nit?

"Now get them two onions off the window ledge. Peel it. Then chop it into small squares."

"You mean dice it small?"

"Whatever. Geez, you. Just chop it into small bits, so it don't feel all slimy in the mouth when you eat it."

Now you might think the two women will start scrapping at the cutting board, but nah. Mostly it's all in fun.

"Get that big pot from the pantry. Wipe it out real good. I don't want no spider shit or fly eggs in it.

"And while you're in there, bring out the deep frying pan for the bread."

"Wimmin's bread?" The words just blurt from Violet's mouth, kind of like a ketchup bottle fart.

Though instead of spraying all over your best tee shirt, Violet laughs.

"Your father would smack you upside the head if you dared put raisins in his bannock."

Walter shouts over Dan and Jim (who marvel at how Miggy's knees have recovered), "So will I!"

"Now grab two sticks of celery. Make sure you wash it up real good. Then chop it up into tiny bits, like the onions."

Violet preps the celery. The recipe writes itself onto a card her brain files.

"Now scrub a half dozen medium potatoes. Just like you scrub your nails after working the garden all morning. And pick out the eyes. And cut out every dark spot."

The old lady looks them over. She takes one, slices it in half lengthwise. Slices each half lengthwise again. Lays it flat and slices each half in half the other way. Then chops it crossways into chunks.

"Now you hack the rest of it."

After chopping up the spuds, Violet pours a solid glug of oil into the hot stew pot, whooshes it around before tossing in the onions. "Stir it fast. Stew will taste ugly if you let it brown."

Next Violet adds the potatoes and stirs it in real good.

Next Violet adds the celery and stirs it in real good.

Next she puts in the tomatoes, water, and broth. Mixes it all in real good.

Next she adds three hard jerks of Tabasco®.

Stirs it in. Adds three more.

Pretty soon that stew boils. Violet stirring it up all the while.

Last, she shakes the SPAM® chunks in and gently stirs it into the bubbling vegetables.

The old lady takes the stirring spoon and slurps a mouthful, swirls it over her tongue, smacks her lips. She nods. "Pretty good for your first time. Turn the fire low and cover it up. It'll be ready by the time the bread's fried."

Violet grabs the dry measuring cup from the back of the bottom drawer, the flour and lard from the pantry. It has a tin cup tied to the handle.

The old lady puts the measuring cup in the sink. When Violet pulls out the measuring spoons, the old lady puts them in the sink.

She rolls up her sleeves and counts four handfuls of flour into the mixing bowl. Four handfuls and a little bit more. She pours salt into the palm of her hand, then dumps it onto the flour.

"Let me show you a trick. How much salt you think I put in it?"

"I dunno. Maybe a tablespoon or two?"

The old lady pours about the same amount of salt into her palm. "Now hand me them spoons."

She shakes the salt into the teaspoon measure. "Don't matter how big your hand is, that much salt always make a teaspoon. I put in two. Now you put in two.

"That's a lot of salt, i'nit?"

"Not for your father. He'll shake another spoonful onto it."

Violet heebie-jeebies. Salt always makes her think of tequila. And thoughts of tequila give her dry heaves. Or they did before she left rehab this last time.

"Stir it up real good. Yeah, like that."

The old lady presses a fist-sized dip into the mound of flour. Now she taps a tin cup of lard into the dip.

"You could heat the bread pan and lard it good while I work the dough."

With both hands she kneads it into a ball, adds some water, and kneads it some more.

"You want it soft enough to shape. And you want it about this thick. Too thin and it gets hard enough to break teeth. I'nit, skʷóze??"

Walter waves his uppers over his head. "Ha ha, yeah."

"Anyways. Make it too thick and it don't cook through."

"Like Uncle Don's creamed-filled bread?"

"Yeah. No amount of salt and jam could make it taste good."

The women laugh and shape the dough into palm-sized balls, moosh it down into a t-bone shape, dust it with flour, and stack it on a chipped enamel plate by the spattering lard.

"I tried making dumplings one time. Dumplings instead of bannock. Your father refused to eat it, none of it. Not the dumb-things. What he called them: dumb-things."

Laughs. "Dumb-things, really?"

The old lady nods and cackles.

"Chicken broth stained it all yellow.

"He says, 'How you 'spect me to eat this shit, old woman? Looks like someone pissed on bull balls.'

"'Try it,' I says. 'Just try it. It's dumplings. Like bannock. Just boiled with the stew.'

"So he pokes it with his fork. Pink, pink, pink, like that. Pink, pink, pink. And it's a little sticky. And it's a little spongey. And it's a little yellow. He goes, 'Dumb-things won't stick to my damn fork.'

"I don't wanna eat it, but I made it, so I got to. I made it after all. So I cut into one. Show him inside of it's just bread. Not fried. Not baked. Boiled bread.

"Kinda slick on the outside. Kinda slimy.

"And I bite into it. And chew. And chew. And chew. Like I popped a whole pack of Hubba Bubba® in my mouth."

"O, Mum. Gross!"

"Tch. I know, hey!

"So it gets caught in my throat and won't go down when I try swallowing."

She pinches a dough, and carefully places it on the boiling lard. Then another. "This pan holds two at a time. But you got to make it this size. You don't want it touching, and you want it cooked at the same time.

108

"And you put it in gentle so you don't start a grease fire, and you don't burn your hands. Hot lard burns ugly."

"How long's it take?"

"When you see it bubble up in the middle like that? Turn it over. Should be golden. Not too dark. Not too pale. Golden. Like this one.

"Now grab that big bowl off the table. Wipe it out good."

After inspecting the bowl, the old lady says, "Yeah, like that. Now take about six squares of paper towel. Lay it in the bowl like this." She tongs a bannock and shakes oil off of it. Pats it down with paper towel. Folds another one over it. Grease stains it almost invisible.

The old lady hands the tongs to Violet. Violet mimics her mother's moves. Something she could do since she was maybe five. But how could she learn when her own gums are too busy flapping. That's what Dad would say, i'nit? Stop flapping your gums, girl. And listen.

"Check your stew. Make sure none of it's sticking to the bottom of the pot."

Violet takes the spoon from the old lady.

Sometimes you eat it with rice.

Sometimes you eat it with a can of niblets.

But always with Tabasco®-brand red pepper sauce. Always.

The old man's birthday has passed. Just like him, I guess.

But they put out a bowl of stew and two chunks of bannock for him, like they do every Sunday.

Violet tips her water glass in her father's direction. "Happy birthday, Dad."

Walter tips his can of Pepsi® in his father's direction. "Happy birthday, Pops."

The old lady tips her glass of water in her husband's direction. "Happy birthday, my sx̣ay̓wih."

The old man lifts the bowl of stew to his nose and inhales noisily.

The three living ones gawk at him like they see a ghost. (They do, of course.)

"You don't set out my meal just so I could look at it!"

"Sx̣ay̓wih, I put one out for you every Sunday, and every birthday since you died. Something wrong?"

"Geez, woman, I want to share a meal with my family. Like I've done every other time."

"But you don't usually talk. And you don't look so alive."

He pats Violet's hand. He imagines brushed denim heat rising from her. Gooseflesh paints itself up her arm. "Today's special. My baby girl cooked it."

"O, Dad. I helped a little."

"You did morren that. You'll sleep good tonight. Maybe every night from now on."

The old man shakes salt on his stew and on his bannock. He splurts Tabasco® on his stew.

Then splurts a little more.

He eats loud for a dead guy.

But he eats.

Ingredients

- Two cans of SPAM®, cut into one-inch cubes (Do not use SPORK® or canned corned beef hash, or the old man will have something to say to you!)

- Two small cans of diced tomatoes

- Two small cans of water

- One small can of chicken broth

- Two medium onions, diced

- Two stocks of celery, diced

- Vegetable oil, maybe a quarter cup, maybe a half cup

- Six medium potatoes, cut in one-inch chunks, give or take

- Salt to taste

- Tabasco® sauce, and plenty of it (Use only Tabasco®-brand red pepper sauce or the old man will have something to say to you!)

Method

1. Prepare vegetables and set aside.

2. Pour tomatoes and broth into a mixing bowl. Fill the tomato cans with water, then stir it into the mixing bowl. (Note: for a thinner broth, add a little more water.)

3. Heat a large saucepan over medium heat. Add cool oil. Stir in onions, and cook off volatiles. Do not let the onions brown, or the old man will have something to say to you!

4. Stir in the celery and potatoes. Add the liquid. Stir well. Make sure stew doesn't stick to the bottom of the pan, or the old man will have something to say to you!

5. Cook it till the spuds is mostly done, maybe forty minutes.

6. Gently stir in the SPAM®.

7. Add Tabasco®.

8. Bring to a simmer, cover, stirring occasionally, until it's finished, maybe fifteen minutes.

9. Add more Tabasco®.

10. Serve it with bannock — fried, not baked, or the old man will have something to say to you!

11. Or serve it over rice. If you want the old man to eat it with you, use long grain white rice. If you don't, use any rice you like. Add Tabasco®-brand red pepper sauce to taste.

12. Enjoy it!

A Wager

1

Yellow hiked eight miles to Uncle Chuckie's fish camp to invite him to dinner. On Friday, of all nights. *Normal people, even most of the old ones, got cell phones,* Yellow thought. *I could text a normal person: cum 4 a meal. 6?*

But not his uncle, who, serenaded by River, sat under that fat maple with some lame western story and sweet black tea in a cracked mug.

Walk eight miles. Pull up a chair. Have tea. Listen to a stupid story.

Have a smoke.

Yet another story.

Six came and went.

Night fell fast and hard enough to make the trees groan under its weight.

"Mom's gonna kill me," Yellow said.

———

"Why?" Chuckie said.

"Look at the time. She wanted us to eat like an hour ago."

"O, well," Chuckie said. "I could throw a couple a deer burgers on?"

Yellow scowled, tapping his feet like a woodpecker on meth.

"Smatter? Some place else you got to be?"

"Nah," Yellow mumbled. "I guess not. Not now, anyways."

"Trees told me somethin else."

"Trees?" Yellow said, all cocked brow and sneery sigh.

"Sure. They tell me ev'rythin I need to know. Like one a my nephews planned on getting into some mischief in Vancouver."

Yellow blanched, choked on a breath, and threw up his hands. Chuckie hid behind his cracked mug.

After a time, Yellow said: "Trees! You get all your gossip from trees?"

"No, not all of it. Just the juiciest stuff," Chuckie said.

"Uncle, howm I spost to believe that?"

"I ever lie to you?" Chuckie inhaled deeply, and held his breath.

"All a time." Yellow smiled like he had just snared a rabbit.

"How bout you tell me when you think I lied," Chuckie said.

Yellow paced, lips pursed, shoulders taut. He pointed at his uncle, and gloated at him.

"What about the time you told me Mom's a black bear."

"No, not that one."

"Why not? Cos it's a load of bull?"

"No. It's not my story to tell."

"Not even when you told me it?"

"Yep. Shoulda kept that one to myself."

"I bet you're too chicken to admit you lied."

Chuckie shook his head, topped up his tea, lit a smoke. Had anyone else called him a chicken, Chuckie would have popped him one in the mouth. And the kid had to make a wager, a challenge that Chuckie could not let slide.

He tapped out his smoke into the Nabob can nailed to the maple.

"What's your bet?" Chuckie said.

"I bet you lied about my mom transforming into a bear. And I'm so sure of it, I'll put up my new dip net. Just finished it."

"It any good?"

"At least as good as yours."

"That's pretty big talk, kiddo."

"It's a good one, all right. Even put a carving in the handle. So, yeah, real good. Maybe the best one in the village." Again, the boy gloated. "And when I win this bet, what you givin me?"

"You could keep your net." He laughed through slitted eyes and clenched jaw.

"Right. How bout you pay me a hunnerd bucks when you lose."

"Holy. Cocky kid. That's a lot a money for a dip net. Tell you what. Make it fifty and you got yourself a bet."

"Ezekiel Moses offered me two hunnerd for it."

"Sure he did."

"Yep. Two big ones."

Chuckie thought, *Yeah, two singles, more like.* Chuckie laughed and offered his nephew a smoke from a new pack. They smoked. Yellow tapped ash onto the dirt and ground it in with the ball of his foot.

115

"So, Uncle, how you gonna get yourself outta this one?"

"I'll tell you after we smoke. Now be quiet, you."

As Chuckie smoked he thought of a way he could both keep his word to his sister, and win the wager. The outcome might anger his sister and her boy, but no one would get hurt, and he would almost certainly have a new dip net for his trouble. He smiled. After snuffing his smoke out on a rock, he smooshed the butt into the coffee can. Yellow flicked his butt toward River. It tumbled into cracks between some of River's rounded rocks. Smoke meandered up.

"Pick that up. You wanna start a fire?"

"What could it hurt there? It's nothing but rock, sand, and water."

"If even one spark got up into the air, this whole mountain could go up in flames." Chuckie snapped his fingers. "Like that. Now holster that smart mouth a yours and go get it."

"More like it'll end up in a fish's belly." Yellow slouched toward his discarded smoke, thinking curses he would never say aloud.

"You okay with makin fish taste like ashtray?"

"As if. You worry too much."

"I'd worry less if you acted more like I taught you."

Yellow poked his hand into the crevice and fished around for his still-smoking cigarette butt. A young gopher snake wiggled over his fingers.

"H'ai!" He yanked his hand from the crevice, scraping his knuckles. Blood oozed from his little wounds. Yellow sucked his scraped knuckles.

"You see that? A rattler just bit me."

"Gopher snake. She just danced over you."

"How djoo know?"

"She told me she hadda teach you a lesson."

Yellow pursed his lips and glared at his uncle.

"Don't get mad at me. You threw that cigarette butt. Now get it before somethin bad happens."

Yellow saw black. He jammed his fingers into the cracks between rocks, and with the force of surging River, flipped the ones he could. Before long, both his hands burned with scrapes and tiny cuts agitated by grains of black sand. After some time he found the cigarette butt and squished it into the Nabob can. Chuckie nodded. He saw Yellow's potential, despite his nephew's thick-skulled youth. Yellow, however, looked at his uncle and saw a talking donkey.

"You satisfied now?" Yellow said.

"Almost. There's no point in bein mad at me." Laughing, he gently swatted Yellow's shoulder.

"It was just one butt. It wouldn't of harmed no one."

"You gonna use an ashtray from now on?"

"Guess so."

"Good."

"Now when you going to admit the truth about my mother and gimme my fifty bucks?"

"New Moon in three nights. On that night, paint your face black, wear your darkest jeans and shirt, and your quietest shoes. Not them things you got on."

"Hey. Don't knock my kicks. They're Air Jordans. These babies cost a bundle."

"I don't know what you young people think, wasting money like that."

"Look at you. All of a sudden you in charge of my family's money? Anyways, what them Tony Lamas cost you? Six hunnerd? Seven?"

"Eight-fifty, but that's different. A bull rider's gotta look good on that bull."

"When you ever ride a bull with them fancy boots on?"

"That's not the point." He thought about giving his nephew another cigarette. Then he thought again.

"Anyways, I need to look good when I'm ballin." Yellow became the picture of Jordan stuffing the net. "Girls like it."

His smile faded. His arms dropped to his sides.

"Hey, Uncle, why I have to dress like Night?"

"Answered your own question, i'nit?"

"Do you even have fifty bucks?"

Chuckie slid a tattered fifty-dollar bill from his wallet and slapped it onto his nephew's thigh, perhaps harder than necessary.

"Put it under the door mat. Tomorrow you bring my new net and hang it beside my old one."

Yellow obeyed.

2

Three nights later the two met where an old deer trail forked from the Petani Road. Both men passed for shadows. Both walked with such stealth the air around them didn't stir, so quietly they didn't disturb the chorus of crickets. Chuckie put his hand flat on his nephew's chest and touched his nose to Yellow's.

"We can head back now, if you want, Nephew." His voice was barely audible over the crickets, but Yellow heard every word as clearly as his own thoughts. "Your mother be mad if she ever finds out."

"Don't matter," Yellow said, as quietly as his uncle. "She's always mad at me about somethin, anyways."

"She's not."

"Seems like it."

After walking the trail for some time, the men stopped short of a clearing. Now he knew where he stood. His family picked soapberries here, had for hundreds of years. For as long as he could remember, he, his mother, and grandmother camped here every summer, picking berries for days and days. Chuckie pointed into the clearing. The cricket chatter stopped, their song interrupted by another, a prayer in nłeʔkepmxcín, sung in his mother's soft voice. Yellow's heart raced, and his feet urged him back the way they'd come. He pulled close to his uncle, squeezing the big man's forearm. His eyes went wide and round as Owl's, and refused to close; he bit his lip, holding back the scream trying to burst from him when he made out the shape of a dress, hung neatly from a dead fir branch about four feet from the clearing's edge. Chuckie's hand clamped on Yellow's quivering shoulder. He raised the *shhh* sign with his free hand, and admonished Yellow with a look that penetrated the thick night, then he turned away. Yellow edged forward, past the dress, and gaped into the small clearing, stamped flat by generations of deer bedding on it. His naked mother unrolled deer hides and spread them over the clearing floor. Yellow closed his eyes, tight, trying to fill his head with pictures of anything but his naked mother bent over a bunch of deer hides. And failed. She grunted loudly. He peeked as she beat a bush with a long, lacquered stick.

Berries, twigs, and leaves rained down on her and the deer hide mats she had laid. She dropped the stick.

She looked heavenward and cried out, "X̱əƛ́scéme! X̱əƛ́scéme! X̱əƛ́scéme!"

She peeled the skin from her breast, revealing thick black fur. Yellow's eyes would not close. She pulled her hair, and with it her face, revealing a snapping black bear's head. He could not turn away. A glistening black bear, standing on her hind legs, stood over his mother's shed skin. Yellow's feet would not carry him off.

The bear raised her forepaws to the heavens and roared at New Moon. One by one, that bear shook the bushes so hard that less ripe berries, smaller branches, and leaves fell to the ground. Most missed the hides. As soon as the trees stood bare, she devoured everything, unripe and ripe berries, twigs, leaves, and unfortunate bugs who became entangled in her threshing claws.

In short order she had hoovered the ground around the soapberry bushes as clean as the spot on a carpet vacuumed by an Electrolux® salesperson. With nothing left to eat, she put her forepaws over her eyes and cried.

Chuckie tugged on Yellow's shirt and led him down the mountain. Once they were safely at the Petani Road, some of the myriad questions bubbling inside Yellow boiled over his lips. Chuckie held his breath, nodded here, frowned there. At last, Yellow sucked in a loud breath and fell silent. Chuckie said nothing for quite some time. Yellow gritted his teeth and tapped his feet in time to his racing heart.

"Well, what you got to say for yourself? Why'd you show me that? Tell me, Uncle. You owe me that much."

"I owe you nothin. I tried gettin you to back off. I showed you the truth. That was our wager." He chewed his lower lip. "Anyways, it's your mother's story to tell, if she chooses to tell it." He pasted on his just-won-the-blackout-bingo smile. "As for me? I'll rest a while, then break in my new dip net. You comin? You could have my old one. It's still pretty good."

He patted Yellow's back, and started the long walk back to his house.

Yellow, a shadow among shadows, stood stone-still, rattle-snake-glaring at the darkness his uncle had disappeared into.

3

Yellow paced the length of his small room until first light,
when his mother returned. He listened to her fitful sleep.
At eight, three full hours later than usual, he crept into the
kitchen, fired up the wood stove, pulled from its hiding place
the pint jar of grease – a jar of liquid gold that had cost him
a half-dozen sides of smoked fish – a can of lard, white flour
and baking powder, and began fixing breakfast for his mother.
Grease-covered bannock, sċwén in fish broth, green tea, and
Tang, a feast suitable for Christmas.

The smell of bannock frying teased his mother awake.
Her tummy grumbled, and a cramp as hard as a transition
contraction doubled her over. She wrapped herself in her terry
robe, slid her feet into her fur-lined moccasins and shuffled
into the kitchen.

"You didn't go to so much trouble for me, did you?" she said.

"And why wouldn't I?"

"Of all days you pick to spoil me, you choose the one I am
cursed with a sick stomach."

"Just a sick tummy, Mom?" He leered at his mother. "Look.
Your favourite: grease on bannock. How could you say no to
this feast?"

Yellow waved the steaming plate under her nose. She grabbed
her stomach and moaned, then dropped into her chair at the
head of the table. He sniggered into his cuff, set his mother's
plate in front of her. Grease, a treat whose aroma always filled
her with joy, now sent her stomach tumbling like a car off a cliff.

He placed a bowl of fish broth beside the bannock, and wafted its rich, salty aroma toward his mother's nose.

"I must of eaten something that disagreed with me."

"Maybe a whole lot of somethin that disagreed with you, i'nit?"

"What you getting at?"

"Gettin at? I just wanted to surprise you. Treat you special, the way you deserve."

She tensed, and willed her stomach still. Her eyes narrowed. She scanned his face, his body, his small movements and easy grace as he fussed over his kitchen work. He must have had another growth spurt and become a man overnight, as lithe and sly as his uncle.

"We got no lemon juice, but I hope you like it anyways."

Her stomach pushed tears out the corner of her eyes.

"Somethin wrong?" Yellow said. His mother shook her head, and groaned.

He sagged, and then removed his mother's meal from her sight. He brought her a mug of green tea and kissed the top of her head. Her stomach rumbled, shaking her. She farted a fart that made Uncle Chuckie's most belligerent beer fart seem rosy and spring-like. Its stink tsunamied the small kitchen, knocking Yellow back two full steps.

Another fart rumbled past her tightly clenched buttocks. She moaned, excused herself and scuttled off to the bathroom. She slammed the door behind her, hiked up her robe and dropped onto the seat.

Yellow carefully scraped the grease from his mother's bannock back into the jar, then placed it back in its hiding place.

He put on a Hank Williams record. He cleaned up the kitchen, and put away the food; cold bannock was still bannock. Then he sat at his place at the table and watched the bathroom door like a hunter in a duck blind. Waxen jasmine scent wafted out from under the bathroom door. Every now and then his mother moaned, mumbled, or cried out.

His mother wept into her palms. (*He knows.*) She sat on the toilet until the jasmine scented candle's wick tab was all that remained of it (*he knows*), until her buttocks and right leg fell asleep (*he knows*), and then she sat a while longer.

After quite some time, her stomachache eased. She leaned against the vanity and tried to wash away her grief. Yellow stood at the bathroom door as it opened. He took his hang-over-coloured mother by the arm and led her to her place at the kitchen table like she was a frail old woman.

"Too much soapberries'll do that to you, i'nit?" he said.

"Soapberry? What do you think you know?"

Yellow recounted all he had seen the night before, telling her everything, excluding his uncle's part.

"So you know everything, then?"

"No. I got two questions: why you transform? You like a werebear, or somethin? And will it happen to me, too?"

She laughed. "Such a man, you! Go make us a big pot of tea and I'll tell you my story."

He put the kettle on and brewed a big pot of salal tea. Lips pursed, she considered her story and how best to tell it. He tore open a package of saltines and dumped some onto a saucer.

Her story came to life in her mind. He filled her favourite cup and put it and the crackers on the table beside her.

"Kʷukʷscémxʷ," she said. She nibbled a corner of a saltine. Crumbs flaked from it. She licked the pad of her thumb and daubed them up, scraped them off on the edge of her plate.

Aside from his mother's delicate nibbling, and the wood stove's occasional pops and ticks, they sat in silence. Yellow cupped his mug, but didn't drink. His mother turned invisible. Yellow waited. Time passed. His mother became visible again, and refilled her mug.

"When I was a little girl, an old witch had a large farm at the edge of our village. You know that place as the Hollow."

Yellow shuddered, and squeezed his cup a little tighter.

"Anyways, she had the finest fruit trees in the whole canyon. She grew the blackest, juiciest, sweetest cherries you could imagine. You could get enough juice to fill four glasses from one of her peaches. But no one went on her land. They say'd she'd grind you into food for her dogs if she caught you in her gardens. The only ones that went on it was them she hired to pick." She nibbled another cracker and sipped some tea.

"I guess I was about five, and even though I knew better, I sneaked into that witch's orchard and stole a handful of cherries. I gobbled them down and wiped my hands on a fence-post, but my chin was stained black, I guess, cos Mom knew right away what I'd done. She prayed while she scrubbed my face and hands, and then gave me such a spanking, and told me to never do it again. That was the end of it, until that witch's peaches ripened."

She sniffled into a tissue. Drew a deep breath.

"Instead of sneaking in and grabbing the nearest peach, I went after a big fat one way up high in an old tree. Now I could climb a tree as good as any boy and never worried about falling, so I scramble up that tree like a squirrel. The farther out I go on this branch, the more it bends and creaks. But my watering mouth and grumbling tummy egg me on. All I see is that giant peach, and I don't hear nothing, not until — just as I grab my peach: *Snap!* — I crash to the ground. My prize, lost, even as peaches hail all around me. I get up on my knees and think it's not so bad because I haven't cut myself or broken any bones, and instead of one peach, I got a whole bunch."

Her son, his jaw hung slack, leaned toward her. She peeled his mug free of his white-knuckled grip, one reason she never could tell him stories before putting him to bed.

"But before I could pick them up, I'm swallowed by a shadow so cold I could see my own breath. When I look up, it's into that old witch's angry face.

"'You destroyed my best peach tree,' she says.

"'I'm sorry. It was on accident,' I say, and start to cry.

"'Nothing happens on accident,' she says to me, real mean.

"'Anyways, it's just one branch and a few peaches,' I say.

"'My best tree. My best peaches,' she sneers. 'And you killed it.'

"She looms over me like a snake about to strike a mouse, pulls me to my feet and gives me a brain-rattling shake. Shakes me so hard my insides vibrate long after she lets go of me.

"'I think you're a little bear,' she says, 'clumsy with greed, and a slave to those worms thriving in your covetous belly,

126

so each month, even through winter, on the night with no moon you will transform into a bear and gorge on whatever food you find outside, until sunlight cracks the horizon.'

"Her words worked on me like poison. As she says them I feel something change inside of me."

Yellow's mother took a sip of tea. She failed to meet her son's curious eyes.

"You know, Mom, this sounds a lot like one of Uncle's stories. If I hadn't of seen it myself, I wouldn't of believed you."

His mother nodded and took a deep breath.

"My brother does know how to tell a tale, i'nit?" she said. She forced her eyes onto her son's. "I wish you hadn't of seen who I am inside."

"That's not you. It's something some old witch put on you."

"No, it's me all right. She just brought it out for everyone to see," she said. "Mom told me I had to go and beg that old hag to take her curse off me. But I chickened out. Anyways, that winter got colder than any winter before. People starved to death, and that old witch stayed warm and full in her house. Come spring, we saw no sign of her. No slaves pruning her trees, no smoke from her chimneys, none of her dogs killing squirrels and chipmunks. No signs of life at all.

"So after a village meeting, Chief and a couple of our best hunters check on her. They find her dead on her kitchen floor. Seems the old witch ate so much preserves she exploded, popped like a balloon, painting her walls and floor with cherries, peaches, apples, and everything else she'd put up."

"Shouldn't her curse of died with her?"

"I wish! But it don't work like that. They say'd her cellars was crammed full of preserves, most so old even bears and worms wouldn't eat it. Chief and them boxed up some of the good jars for us to eat. Then, as soon as they stepped off that old witch's land, a huge rumble shook Canyon. They dropped them preserves and ran for their lives. And just in time, too."

She smiled. Her son, a full-grown man an hour ago, sat across from her, a wide-eyed four-year-old.

"What happened? They live?" Yellow said.

"O, yes! They all lived. The ground opened up and swallowed everything that witch owned, and then it died. Chief and them's hair turned white, and they never slept again, not for the rest of their lives."

"No way. They'd of died from been awake so long."

"We buried the last of them not five years ago. Old Travis John. Anyways, that's why I transform into a bear on the night of the New Moon. I would of told you one day, when I thought you ready. I wish your uncle would of waited, and let me tell you in my own time."

"Don't blame Uncle Chuckie, Mom. I bet him my new dip net that he made up that story about you transforming into a bear."

"Holy! Must be betting with my brother invites bad magic, i'nit? Maybe you're a witch."

"Mom! Don't even joke like that."

The Sunshine Rainbow
Peace Ranch

So some time ago them dippy-hippies took over that dead
settler's shack. Old guy. Kept to himself. Called himself Harvey
Blackwater. Poached deer sometimes. Stole a cow one time.
One of Leon Jimmie's. Leon drags a cop to Harvey's squat.
Leon says to that cop, "There. That cow's mine."

Cop says, "How can you tell? Where's your brand?"

That Harvey Blackwater says, "Nope. Ol' Suzie here's my cow.
Bin takin care of her for some time. She got no tag. No brand.
No collar. Nothin to say she belonged somewheres else. Looked
at the board in front the post office. No one lookin for a lost
cow there, neither. Anyways, I give Suzie her name. I give her a
warm place to sleep. Inside with me.

"I take her on a long walk two times a day. Morning, we walk
down River. Look for jade and other valuables River gives us.
And after supper every night we walk the bush. Little cooler then.

———

"Before bed I brush her out and sing her lullabies. Sometimes read her scriptures, too.

"We're good, God-fearing Christians, so Suzie belongs to me."

That cop nods, says, "Harvey here makes good sense. He's a good Christian, raising his cow to be a good Christian too. And Harvey here has the cow in his possession, on his land."

Leon's wife Eloise always tells him to breathe and think before talking out loud. That Harvey Blackwater parks his '47 International Harvester on a patch of land just north of Three Mile. Puts a six-acre fence around it. Puts a big red barn on it. Puts a two-room shack on it. Puts a fancy gate in front of it. Puts a fancy sign on the fancy gate. *Crown* looks it over and tells him and us that he earned that land fair and square.

Not so nice now. Swaybacked barn roof. Swaybacked shack roof. Fence trampled in places, crushed by snow in others, barbed wire snipped in others. Once some guy cuts ten or twelve feet of barbed wire to tie his muffler back onto his car, but most of that wire snipped because Harvey Blackwater strung it.

And now he rustles Leon Jimmie's milk cow.

"It's my cow. I got papers to prove it."

Harvey Blackwater pours black coffee into a chipped, blue enamel mug. He doesn't offer one to Leon or the cop.

Cop says, "It's a cow. All cows look alike."

That Harvey Blackwater, squatting on *Crown Land*. Like any *Crown* ever set foot on it, hey? Lots of crows, but. Definitely crow land, that.

Cop says, "I think you want to use the justice system to steal a hardworking man's cow."

Harvey Blackwater snorts wetly and clears his throat. Sounds like a rabid coyote Leon come across out hunting that one time. Harvey Blackwater belches.

"I think you are wasting my time, as well as the time of this hardworking gentleman."

Cop says, "Leon Jimmie, I have more important things to do than help you solve a civil dispute. If you are so sure this fine gentleman has taken your cow, take him to court. Let a judge decide who owns what here."

Leon raises a finger to speak.

The cop shuts him up with his upraised hand. He says, "Leave now and I won't arrest you for mischief and trespass."

Leon can take a hint.

You don't need to ask Leon twice. He walks stiff and formal, stopping inside that fancy gate, and grrrs, "Die a slow, painful death, Harvey Blackwater."

Maybe Leon Jimmie would have wished something different for Harvey Blackwater, if he'd known about Harvey's cancer.

Harvey Blackwater passed on his squat, Suzie mindlessly chewing her straw bedding, and her cud. One day she broke out of that squat and wandered along the highway, till that cop stopped her, and got her back to Harvey's place.

That was spring of '71.

Later that summer, not long after that cancer kills Harvey Blackwater, fella name of Morris Jim comes to town.

Good Indian name, that Jim.

This Morris Jim's about as white as them səmséme? get, but.

From up Chilcotin way, I think, that name Jim, not this Morris Jim.

From up Chilcotin way, I think.

Not so much around here, though.

That Morris Jim brings thirty friends, too. Thirty dippy-hippies, them friends.

Sometimes them thirty friends feels like three hundred, but.

Yeah, they took over that barn.

Patched that raggedy old fence.

Sheesh, them hippies even put a new door on that outhouse.

Didn't dig a new pit for it, but.

They got that Teit book, hey. Knows a lot about them Indian ways, that James Teit. Yeah, that Scotchman settled out nkəmcín way. Them dippy-hippies build themselves one authentic Indian sʔístkn.

Just like that Teit shows it.

Not many left to say how right that Teit book was. Some just babies then. Old now. Old ones say he makes a pretty good Indian for a white guy. Old ones say he understands our ways. Respects our ways.

But them dippy-hippies, they got hold of that Teit book. Build themselves that sʔístkn. Thirty dippy-hippies snoring and screwing around the smoke hole. Looks like rag rug the old womens sew. Anyways, that's what they say.

Some sneak out there to watch them womens.

Some sneak out there to watch them dippy-hippies screw.

Crazy stuff that.

Cray-zee.

Dress in striped bell bottoms, fringed fake leather vests.
Even them dippy-hippy womans not wearing shirts. Most wearing headbands, some beaded, some woven.

Some southwestern styles.

Some northern plains.

Some Northwest coast.

Most a jumble of styles.

Most mean nothing.

And all the wrong colours.

Lotta wolf and eagle motifs.

Lotta flowers, sunflowers, sunburst. Medallions lazy stitched or glued. Some on gold chains. Some on silver. A few beaded chains.

Them dippy-hippies put more work in a month than that squatter Harvey Blackwater in most of the years he squats.

Got that authentic corrugated iron roof.

Got that authentic tin chimney.

Got that authentic oak door.

Got that authentic brass door knob.

Paint big picture on barn. Got them cigar-store Indians smoking pipes with bear and deer and wolf and eagle. Got them perfect trees. Got them little blue birds from *Cinderella* singing "This Land Is Our Land." Words in fluffy clouds. And a sun painted sorta Haida style, but Cheyenne pink and greasy yellow.

And painted that authentic sign on it. Red. Black. White. And chartreuse. Fucking chartreuse paisley.

Sign says: "Welcome! Sunshine Rainbow Peace Ranch."

Sheesh! Them dippy-hippies call that squat of theirs Sunshine Rainbow Peace Ranch.

That ranch on a side-a the mountain. Steep, that land. Narrow part of the canyon. Gets enough light to grow some rocks. Not much else.

The Sunshine Rainbow Peace Ranch.

And that Morris Jim walk through town in nothing but a breechcloth and bone breast plate, and that headband with giant eagle medallion.

Wind, ever tricky that Wind, whooshes that breechcloth onto breastplate. Wind rattles that breastplate like a bone wind chime. Sounds pretty good.

Now that Morris Jim got a spaeks? on him. Wind tickles Morris Jim's nut sack. Yeah, I know what you're thinking right now, but that's too easy.

And that Morris Jim reads from a black book:

> "The Earth, my god, how
> it quakes. And swallows
> little cars and littler peoples."

And the street fills with people. They pour from the pub like it's on fire. And pretty quick cops pull up. Got that Spotface from the east and that Constable Howe from the west. Two of the meanest cops in the world, them two. Boxing him in. Their cherries painting him and everyone close cherry red. No sirens. Howe has his nightstick out before he leaves the car. I guess you could say that nightstick's like a second middle finger. Howe's nightstick middle finger silences the crowd, but not Morris Jim. He smiles like a guy with tickled balls and reads some more:

> "And I beckon Her, 'O, Mother, O, Earth.
> Shake off these encroaching fleas.

Lead me by the cock to a trough
where I might feed.'
And on a thought I skate
to Venus, then to Mars."

Howe says, "I am arresting you for public drunkenness, public indecency, disturbing the peace, possession, production, or distribution of obscene material."

Morris Jim says:

"Obscene? This Earth Mother
sculpted form, her labial caress
of Love's grand hard on
spewing love, maddening love."

"That's it. You're resisting arrest."

Morris Jim says:

"Arrest my immaculate cock
my fevered conception."

Howe and Spotface don't even wait to get Morris Jim up dump road. If Morris Jim's beating happened now, you could watch it on the Google®, or the YouTube®. But those days phones don't fit in your pocket. And they don't take pictures. And they don't sext. Anyways, they screwed into the wall, so you can't take them outta the house. Sometimes I miss them old days. Maybe not everything, but old ways of using the phone, yelling at your caller, and not have everyone on the street know you owe bank three payments.

Howe cracks Morris Jim a good one in the kidney. "You wanna play a dirty little savage. You get treated like a dirty."

Whap.

"Little."

Thwack.

"Savage."

Howe and Spotface believe they're North-West Mounted Police officers determined to solve Sir John A's Indian problem. Who'm I kidding, all policemen think they still have to solve his Indian problem.

"I am the bulletproof, chokered Indian.

Choked."

So no one sees Morris Jim around. No one sees the prison transfer truck come around either. Maybe one week. Maybe two.

Old lady Martha John sees him first. That old woman sees everything. She sees your kid peeing in The Town Butcher's mailbox. She sees Eileen and Marvin scrapping in the alley. But who hasn't, hey? Maybe one day Marvin'll get a lick in. Maybe one day he'll learn to keep his trap shut. But probably not.

She sees your kid steal the hubcaps off the mayor's Caddie. No one would've known he paid seven hundred dollars for them if he hadn't bragged about how much he paid every time he had Tom Collinses at the Legion. Cops show up, give the mayor a case number for his insurance claim. They gotta solve the Indian problem, and now the dippy-hippy problem, so they don't have time to chase after some rich asshole's hubcaps.

Now your kid trades them for a half gallon of plonk from town mechanic Arthur Wainwright the Third, who sells them back to the mayor for $150. Mayor brags he got them for a steal from Arthur, who pays your kid a half gallon of plonk to steal them. I guess that's capitalism.

Anyways, old Martha John says Morris Jim left Saint Jude's that morning. Out the backdoor. The one they use to take body parts to the incinerator, to put used needles and stuff in the can they keep locked.

Next time Morris Jim comes to town he has on dirty jeans and his chest wrapped in bandages. He reads from a red book: "The mummy engulfed me in her fractious womb–"

He moans and hugs his chest. He wheezes, draining what little colour left in his skin. ". . . and dropped me, sans chivalry, on my once immaculate cock . . ."

Uncle Chuckie got back from camp last night. Hazel, the '61 Chevy Impala ss 409, brings he and Edna into town for breakfast and groceries. She sits patiently in the street, watching old Martha John watch town from her third-floor perch.

Morris Jim races to Hazel and kneels beside her right rear quarter panel. He strokes it. "I've talked to crows, and a vulture or two, but never to a car, not one like you."

Agnes the waitress, like old Martha John sees everything going on in town, hears about it too. But usually keeps it to herself. She says, "Hey, Chuck, that dippy-hippy's hitting on your car."

"Think he's gonna hump 'er?"

"I'd like to see him try it," Edna says. "I'll put him back in the hospital faster than you can say filthy hippy."

Agnes fills their coffee cups. "Just when you think this town can't get any crazier, hey?"

Chuckie says, "Aw, he's just a lovestruck puppy. I'll set him straight."

Chuckie cracks his knuckles. Stretches his fingers. Balls his fists. Stretches his fingers. Holsters his hands in his jeans' front pockets. Soft words. Hard fists.

Morris Jim doesn't lift his chamois fingers from Hazel's side. "You know your Hazel has an angelic soul."

"Yeah, I guess you could say that."

"The heavens speak to me through her soul. She's who I envisioned on my vision quest."

"You do know them visions and them peyote hallucinations are two diff'rent things, yeah?"

"The pay-oot was exceptional. Got it from an Indian shaman near Yuma."

Glassy-eyed smile, an idjut still high on that Yuma peyote.

"What once was thine now is mine.

The grand orator, the Great Mystery has shown me a sign."

"You telling me your *needs* is more important than Hazel's or mine? Anyways, she don't belong to anyone."

"I can pay, if money's your thing."

Chuckie thinks how he could spend that dippy-hippy's money.

"I could take your cash, but she'll just come back home."

"She says she likes me. She likes me."

"Hey hee. Hazel? She likes everyone. Doncha, my girl?"

But he's sorta cute. Got a sweet little butt. Maybe I want to take him for a ride. Did you think to ask me? It's my chassis. They're my plush leather seats.

"Gwan then, take that séme? for a spin. And make sure he washes his stink ass offa your plush leather seats, hey?!"

Morris Jim flinches.

"She loves you. You should reward her by letting her go!"

Chuckie draws his right and curls the fist's first fold. "Time you moved along there, budz."

The fist closes. Chuckie's giant, scarred knuckles itch to taste blood. Hazel honks.

Chuckie re-holsters his hand. "Sorry, my girl."

> "You can lament your loss
> or embrace it, its cost
> and let our love grow
> and come and come and come."

"Ain't up to me. You hurt her one little bit, one little ding, one fleck of paint outta place, and I will hurt you."

So off they go, Hazel and Morris Jim. That dippy-hippy, stiff-armed as a European driving a fancy sports car, steering Hazel this way and that like a baby with one of them toy dash-boards attached to their stroller. Lucky for him, Hazel makes all of them engine noises. If Chuckie has to clean dippy-hippy spit of Hazel's dash and windshield — best not think too long on that ugliness. So off they go, east, away from the sunset. Chuckie mutters all the cuss words he saves for them hammer-his-thumb-instead-of-the-nail moments. "So this must be what Cuckold Harry feels like."

Kinda funny how you can sleep with a bud's wife and still call him *friend,* i'nit?

Now Cuckold Harry has an interesting story that ends with his suicide. I could tell you more, but nah.

Chuckie tells it better, anyways.

Edna, pushed back by the glower emitting from the deep of Chuckie's insides, says, "Agnes put your meal under the heat lamps."

Almost as fast as Edna says them words, Agnes appears with Chuckie's meal. New eggs. New hash browns. Three fresh rashers of bacon. Three sausages he hadn't ordered. And a fancy paper umbrella stabbed into a chunk of peeled orange.

"Whoa! Heat lamp must be magic. Meal looks fresh."

When Agnes smiles, her face transforms into an obsidian carving. Agnes isn't as dark as obsidian, but she's as hard.

"Hazel's a little petulant today, i'nit?"

"Nah, she's downright ornery. Like a fourteen-year-old girl."

Agnes and Edna laugh because Chuckie only talks like this when there's a séme? around. And one sits at the lunch counter, a trucker from The Loops on his run to Big Town. This trucker has a thing for one of the waitresses, so he makes town his rest stop, just three hours into his run. Pretty good chance he wouldn't zip along the Coque, if it existed then, like every trucker does nowadays. And that waitress thinks this trucker, a stinky worm of a man with breath like ass, should crawl back into his crypt and stay there. He orders toast and coffee when that waitress is off. He asks, "When's the girl's next shift?" And asks again five minutes later. The girl has a name. We call her Babe because she's the youngest waitress old Sinister Snook ever hired. Her parents call her Babe because she's their youngest kid and it's her name: Babe. Anyways, Chuckie, all pouty and grumpy, has nothing interesting to say, unless you like a man's pouty-grousing.

So. Back to Morris Jim, still thinking he has control of
Hazel. They motor along Highway 16 at seventy miles an hour.
Hazel screeches off 16 onto Bark Creek Road. For a land yacht
Hazel straightens corners like a Highways engineer. Morris
Jim yanks the steering wheel hard left. And nothing happens.
Pumps, then stomps the brake pedal. And nothing happens.
Yoinks the key from the ignition. And nothing happens.

"What the hell, Hazel?! What the unholy hell?!"

*Human. I invited you on this ride. If you don't want to go
where I take you, feel free to hop out. Any time.*

Now Morris Jim thinks on this a minute: Maybe I am too
hard on her. Maybe I should loosen up. It'd be so much easier
if I had a handful of pey-oot, and some of Sweet Sue's magical
mushroom powder. "No. It's cool. It's groovy."

Then stop holding my steering wheel so tight.

"Tight! Right! Erotic might!

You and me, Babe, Outasight!"

In an instant, Morris Jim is as free as his lies to his dippy-
hippy minions. He could camp in a furnace, walk safely
through a cougar den (not them Big Town cougars, or them cats
Mercury transformed into pretend Mustangs), walk across hot
coals, bounce police-fired bullets (they weren't even rubber
in them days) off his chest. He lets the wheel go. He stands on
the seat. The wind at seventy-five miles per hour doesn't blow
him back. Trees to the left and right blur into an infinite three-
dimensional impressionistic painting of a fast-moving tree river.
Bird calls, songs, and trills blend into the lows of cattle, and the
occasional car horn honk and catcall. Nature's song on speed.

Every now and then a bug splats onto his face. And it stings like a rubber bullet, but Morris Jim wouldn't know that, would he?

So he balances on top of the front seat like he's hanging ten. Singing songs loud into the wind. Words blow back into his face, stinging like his mother's acid-tongued diatribes. In the wind. True freedom.

"I love you, Hazel, you angelic automobile."

O, brother. Another human mistakes an erection for love.

"No, not a hard on. It always looks like this. What can I say? Curse of the well-endowed."

As if.

Morris Jim glides to Hazel's trunk, folds himself into a flawless lotus position as he lowers himself onto it.

Her whitewalls strain against their beads as she straightens the 18-Mile esses. If she had brows, they'd be so furrowed. That Morris Jim's butt doesn't scooch any which way. And his posture is as perfect as a statue's. Now transforming into a rock could happen, but usually only the People turn. Morris Jim may be human, but he's not one of the People. No matter how much peyote buttons he pops, no matter how much mushrooms he slurps, no matter how much of that wacky tabacky he smokes, Morris Jim will never be one of the People.

Hazel's tach pushes closer to the red. Dust specks catch fire and turn to dust ash when it flies over the exhaust manifold.

Morris Jim, his arms spread wide, hair blown back, shouts, "Haha hee hee I am invincible; nothing can hurt me!"

Hazel chokes on her carbs and inhales pure gas fumes. I guess when you've hit max speed, you've hit max speed.

Now Hazel's exhaust runs black with some blue, and not like that Superman's hair. Chuckie will have to rebuild her engine. Send it out and get it ported and blueprinted. Replace her manifolds. Rebuild her carbs. He hates rebuilding carbs. So if she can't go any faster . . . she can . . . *SCREEEEEEEEEEEEEEEEEECH!*

Not to a full stop. Boiling water gurgles past the radiator cap.

Morris Jim, except for the slow rise and fall of his chest, hasn't moved.

What's it gonna take to get you off my damn trunk?

"I can't. You and I share a cosmic bond the Great Maker alone can break."

Hazel guns it and she aims at the two-hundred-foot Douglas fir at 22-Mile. The one with thousands of tobacco ties strung to it. Some say that tree's as old as the People. Some say tobacco ties hang all the way up to its tip. Old ones, them ties. Government engineer tapped a Day-Glo orange ribbon onto it, and that ribbon isn't a prize. No, that ribbon says that tree's got to go. Something about safety. Something about maybe one day they cut out that curve and make road safer. *O, yeah? Suck on this, cosmic bond.*

Hazel speed-shifts, zero to forty-five in three seconds. She's tired and needs a rest, maybe an oil change, maybe an ice bath, maybe a mani-pedi. For sure she needs something.

She drifts around the tree and chokes on the dust she throws up. Pebbles and stones like shotgun pellets chew bits of bark off the lodgepole pines standing across from the Douglas fir.

Morris Jim's butt hangs precariously over the left rear quarter panel.

"I am the inertia king; I withstand ev'rything."

Hazel mumbles along at thirty miles an hour. *I need a plan, dammit.*

"Great Maker watches over us. Great Maker rewards perfect love."

And just how is it you know what xeʔɬkʷúpiʔ thinks, silly two-legged?

"He speaks to me. He speaks through me. My poems are His words spoken through me."

As if. Anyways, what makes you think xeʔɬkʷúpiʔ is a man? For all you know, they're an Impala, or Chevy II.

"Yeah, yeah yeah. Or gazelle, or Guernsey, or Morgan. Maybe even a woman."

Too bad you weren't as pretty inside as you are outside.

Morris Jim beams. He stands and two-steps in place, waving an invisible eagle feather fan. Dancing like an old man and an old woman, sheesh.

"I am the Emperor Ming; I rule over things!"

Yeah, and I'm Dale Arden. Fla-ash. Ooo whoooo.

Hazel squeezes closed eyes she doesn't really have. Her grill twists into a strained grimace. Gravel grapeshots behind her. Morris Jim stands. Dusted Wind should sandblast his smug face. But no, Wind caresses his face's pretty skin. Wind wants to kiss his pretty lips. Wind wants to have epic sex with Morris Jim. Wind wants to hear the epic love song he writes in her honour. Maybe Wind spends too much time reading *Tiger Beat* and *Circus* and *Creem*. She confuses Morris Jim with that other fellow. Wind's usually so much smarter. At 26-Mile, a hairpin turn named Death, a curve so tight only a pair of side-by-side sixty-foot spruce trees separates one side of it from the other, marks the start (or end, I guess) of the switchback up to the Frontenback Silver Mine. Someone named them two trees Lulu's Sisters, some miner whose scoliosis or flat feet or bone spurs in his heels kept him out of WWII.

What makes you think a man named them?

"I am the gravity king; only a man can name things."

Hazel has a million ways to respond to Morris Jim. Maybe more. But why waste valuable words and energy on a guy who won't hear you, hey?

Mountain goats stop and put tobacco ties on them spruces before climbing that road in winter. That road so challenging they tram them ores down to their private ferry dock. Miners climb into them ore carts and ride them to and from their shifts. Back in the late-'50s the crew bus, driven by grossly hungover Julian O'Rourke, missed a corner, blueberry pancaking the bus and crew some three hundred feet below. Nothing but air. Straight down.

The story about the wildcat strike and ensuing massacre is another great one best saved for another day. And I tell it better than Chuckie. Better than most, I guess.

So that Morris Jim stands, arms stretched out to the sides, legs spread wide enough to sit on a bull's back. His bell bottoms bloat and snap. And Wind tickles him with a million little kisses. Everywhere.

His hard on rages, bound by his jeans.

Hazel drops down to third, tach jumps to the red line.

Her 409 screams. Its exhaust manifold glows white, blue flames dance on top of it. Her radiator blows its cap. The speedo hits 140, bends then breaks trying to hit 160. White smoke blasts out her tailpipes.

Only a miracle will get Hazel and Morris Jim around that tight hairpin.

Hazel doesn't believe in miracles.

"Wind, my lover, wind my concubine, only Hazel's love is stronger than thine."

As Hazel closes in on the blasted rock wall behind Death, she wonders if the last thing she will see is her own tailpipe. She shifts into neutral.

So long dear Chuckie. I fear the mess I leave you will be impossible for even you to fix. Give my regards to Edna. You know I love her too, right?

And back at the café, this time for dinner, Chuckie shivers the exact same way he did the second his mother passed.

He whispers, "No, not you, my baby."

Edna takes his hand and squeezes it tight. She knows Chuckie means Hazel. Maybe she feels it too. Let's give them some alone time, leave them to their sorrow.

And Wind stops kissing Morris Jim. She folds herself up under Hazel's undercarriage and lifts her.

"O, Hazel, I want to fuck you! O, Wind, I want to fuck you!

"I am the copula king; I can link everything!"

With Wind too busy to hear Morris Jim and Hazel lost in prayer, only some magpies, crows, and squirrels, already stunned silent by Hazel's shenanigans, hear Morris Jim's words.

Each one of them gives their head a shake. You don't know what an eyeroll is until a squirrel lays one on you.

And Morris Jim, now wrapped in a greasy bubble, floats above Hazel, outside of Wind.

"Haha! I am the Lizard King; I can do anything!"

He thinks that line's a keeper. Now's not the time to tell him that line's been done.

Morris Jim bubbles off to the safety of the Sunshine Rainbow Peace Ranch. "My followers, my people, will deify me after they hear my tale. Women will fall at my feet and beg me to knock them up."

He doesn't look back. He doesn't expend a single thought on Hazel. Wind's lusty little kisses fade into distant memory. But Morris Jim's hard on rages, a divining rod guiding him back to the ranch. I hope you don't think Morris Jim gets his happy ending.

Now that's a good enough place to end his part of the story.

Airborne Hazel glides toward safety, but Wind can't steer her clear of the Sisters and she can't lift Hazel over them. Hazel thinks she can pass between them. Chuckie won't mind buffing out any scratches she gets, as long as she lands softly on the other side. Her momentum lags, and Wind doesn't have the juice to push her any faster.

Hazel jolts to a stop. The Sisters shudder and groan. Some of their branches snap under Hazel's weight. Wind takes a run at Hazel's backend, but she's squeezed too tight between Lulu's Sisters and Wind can't budge her. Not an inch.

Oil runs from Hazel's oil pan and the tear in the 409's block. The last of her coolant drips from a burst hose. The exhaust manifold, still smoking, has burned a hole in itself.

Wind sought out her man. She didn't even ask his name before lusting on him like a leg-humping lab. She called out to him, "Hey sexy man, your lady love beckons." (Wind has heard almost every bad love poem recited or sung since the Age of Chivalry. She still thinks Guinevere got the shit-end of the stick.)

One of the sisters, the younger of the twins, snaps, "I told you this would happen if we stayed here. I told you no good would come of that road if we let them build it. 'Just wait them out,' you said. 'We'll outlive them,' you said. Now look at us. We have this abomination between us."

Hey! You watch who you call an abomination! She has no *or else,* or she'd deal with them rude sisters.

Wind works herself into a twister and storms south and west because that's the way Morris Jim floated.

I want to be stuck between you bickering old women as much as you want me here. Now just shut up and help me find a way out of this mess.

"Why should we? Your stupidity landed you here."

Idiot trees, listen good. When the man finds me, he will take a chainsaw to your raggedy old bark.

If age actually made you smarter, the old sisters would have all the brain power of Oppenheimer, Einstein, and every other genius of the past eighty years. Even though you probably couldn't tell the difference, the old trees stand struck dumb.

Hazel wonders whether Chuckie can fix her. Hazel wonders what Chuckie will do when he finds her. Maybe you will too, because this story stops right here.

Gramps v The *real* Santa™

This might not be the story you want to hear, but I will tell it anyways. Stay or move on to the next one. I will wait.

Okay then, let's get started.

So this one happens now. And it happens then, maybe 165 years ago, with Gramps and Granny Lanny young and in love, and it happens later, much later. End of the universe later.

Well, Gramps wears Cupid's arrows right where his brains sit. And just so you know, making water with a love arrow straight up his spaeks? isn't easy. Not easy at all. Granny Lanny, on the other hand, takes one in the heart, and that heart has the hots for Ziff, Gramps' brother. Granny Lanny says she can't help herself because the heart wants what the heart wants. No matter how ill, you can't argue that logic. (Unless you're a lawyer not working on contingency.)

I guess this story happens every day of those 165 years, but this is a novella, not some bloated trilogy, not *War and Peace,* and certainly not *Gone with the Wind.* So Gramps has a knack for growing wheat, raising sheep, and singing beautiful songs no one has ever heard before. The one Gramps sings now isn't one of them. He sings the world's second-greatest love song, you know, that one, by the fabulous J. Geils Band, made re-famous in that pretty-good movie *The Wedding Singer,* "Love Stinks." Lucky Gramps can sing it, but if I show you them lyrics, I'd probly need to dodge lawsuits and cease and desist letters. And why let some a-hole lawyers ruin a good story, hey?

Maybe Gramps himself has a heart that wants what it wants. (I guess this is a bit of foreshadowing. Maybe not.) He stabs the earth around a rotting fence post, in time to that ever hummable love song, and wrestles the post from its hole. He has a sturdy 6x6, pressure-treated replacement. Brand new,

and it costs him dear, but amortized over the next twenty or
thirty years, the dang thing is practically free, and he won't
need to dig, augur, and cement in a new one for decades.
Makes that post, like they say in them TV commercials, price-
less. By his own reckoning, Gramps is about 183 years old now.
No matter. He's as spry as a well-preserved thirty-five-year-old.

O, I should probably tell you that Ziff is Gramps' twin. They
share parents. They have similar strong chins, identical eyes —
colour, expressiveness, rakish twinkles, but Ziff has a receding
hairline, thinning hair tied in an annoying old-man ponytail.
Ziff has more lines on his face. And he carries the burden of his
shame, the burden of Granny Lanny's effusive love — emphasis
on the eff — and his failure to impregnate any of the women in
his life. And he walks with a stoop (but he knows James Dean
is dead). Such a stud, that Ziff. But he only shoots blanks.

Gramps dotes on his grandchildren, great-grandchildren,
great-great-grandchildren, etc. So many generations, the older
ones expire — including his own children, six daughters and
seven sons — he loves each new crop of his progeny as much as
the one before it.

Except maybe his own thirteen kids, at least that's how they
feel, felt, will feel.

He loads each generation of grandchildren with gifts and
gewgaws and trinkets from his travels through the past. And
occasionally, something that won't exist until after they've died.
Dinky, a great-grandson, got a Sony PS4® and flat screen TV.
In 1943. Dinky kept it a secret from everyone outside of his
immediate family. As an adult, he helps create Pong® and the

Atari Entertainment System® and a bunch of video games no one's ever heard of.

But don't you dare go pinning angel wings on this old man, all full of love and hardworking as he is. He has sides. He has layers like an ogre-onion, but not like a wedding cake, xeʔłkʷúpiʔ forbid.

So Gramps is about thirty-six when that Anglican preacher introduces him to Christmas, the birthday of that Jesus fellow. Jesus loves everyone except the dark-skinned savages and pagans, and every savage has darker skin tones, and every savage calls that Jesus fellow, or his father, by a name that makes sense to them. Gramps prays to xeʔɬkʷúpiʔ, and the grandmothers and grandfathers who do good things. Still. Xeʔɬkʷúpiʔ

Father Pierre sighs. "But those are pagan beliefs. They're false idols, my child."

Like I have already said, Gramps is thirty-six. Gramps has two parents and they don't call him *my child*. Because everyone knows Gramps and Ziff and their thirteen sibs belong to Dana and Donna Diablo. No point in restating the obvious, hey? Donna names her first son Gramps because she dreams he will walk through time and help raise hundreds, maybe thousands, of grandchildren.

"Well," says Gramps, "that may be true, but as far as I know xeʔɬkʷúpiʔ has no birthday and no death-day. They just is."

"Still not the Father, the Son, and the Holy Ghost."

"Tell me again why them three are one. You ever see that movie *The Three Faces of Eve?* How them three get along?"

Okay, this is 1876, and they haven't even heard of *The Three Faces of Eve* yet. The real Eve herself is born in fifty-one years. This sort of gaffe happens when you live outside of time.

"Are you just thick, my child, or are you trying to get under my skin?"

Gramps shrugs. "I dunno. Curious is all."

"I've a lot to do in preparation of my sermon. I think I shall speak on the Spirit of Christmas."

"You mean Scrooge and them? Read it a long time ago, well I will have read it at some point. Same with the movies. Seen'm all. Some I'll see more than once. And not just at Christmas."

The preacher almost challenges the existence of Scrooge movies. Almost. In 1876 there are no Scrooge movies. They release the first one in twenty-five years. It's the first of maybe a couple a dozen. And that first Scrooge movie shows maybe thirteen years after the first real motion picture. Of course the preacher doesn't know this and won't.

Maybe you didn't know about all them Scrooge movies either. But now you do.

You're welcome.

Almost everyone in the world has read *A Christmas Carol* by 1876, a fact I've just invented. It hasn't the same magic as Clement Clarke Moore's poem, which you read to your children or grand-children before bedtime on Christmas Eve and your mother or grandpa read to you before bedtime on Christmas Eve. Try reading Scrooge before bedtime. Trying keeping your children interested and unscared. Best wait for the movie. Better yet, wait for Alistair Sim in the title role: the 1951 version. Father Pierre knows naught of this, so he ignores Gramps' observation. Such a smart man that Gramps, but the two halves of his brain sometimes fail to commu-nicate with each other. And Father Pierre says, "In a way, I suppose. But not in Dickens' mundane laical manner. Our Lord and Saviour will not tolerate such devilry as ghosts and hauntings, and such claptrap as traversing time in order to learn lessons.

"The spirit of which I speak has nothing to do with Satanic pagan rituals. The spirit of which you speak is base idolatry. The spirit of which you speak violates the first two commandments."

Gramps thinks, What about Matthew 7:12, hey? All y'all overlook your god's own laws. The padre doesn't like his own bible's words thrown back in his face, so Gramps says, "So many rules. No wonder all y'all look so miserable all the time."

"Without rules we live in chaos. Chaos is Satan's domain. Order is godly."

"I see. Maybe it's time for you to get to work on that speech of yours, hey?"

"I'll pray for you, my child."

"You just go ahead and do that, Padre."

Father Pierre rolls his eyes and craps out. He would have Gramps committed to the asylum, but as savages go, Gramps is one of the good ones, one of the few with the potential to be a fine Canadian citizen. Too bad his dark skin doesn't wash off like dirt, hey Padre? So he tolerates Gramps' incoherent ramblings as vestiges of idolatry. That's how he writes it up in his journal. He hopes to write for a living when he's older and has the time. He hopes to write the definitive anthropological study on the nłeʔkepmx people: Fuck Boaz and fuck Tait. Yeesh, such ungodly ejaculations, Padre.

The padre would flog himself if he enjoyed pain.

He would spill his sinful thoughts and blasphemous words in confession, but his god, who's not up there at all, can't give a shit about his creations and wouldn't if it could.

Father Pierre: atheist Anglican preacher.

For most of us, traversing time lets us witness our gaffes, but not necessarily correct them, driving many of us crazy.

Father Pierre hates Christmas. He and his seminary buddies talk about the birth of their saviour and why they put it on 25 December. Tricking savages and pagans into rebranding it to celebrate something their bible knows nothing about — the Christ's actual birthday. Such a life he leads. His burden weighs a little less than Ziff's. But the preacher has much better luck than Ziff, because he drops dead of heart failure on 26 April 1870, three years from now. He prays Santa Claus will overtake Jesus and the day will become about consumerism, mass consumption. "O, God, our Father, through your Son, the beloved Christ, I implore you to let the Holy Spirit guide The *real* Santa™ onto the throne that we know as Christmas — 25 December."

Rather than reach for the sacramental wine, he pulls from the bottle of Buffalo Trace he keeps in his oaken secretary.

The idea of Santa Claus has kicked around since the early nineteenth century, and as early as the third, if you count that scary fellow and patron of children, Saint Nicolas. But Gramps doesn't know this. He won't know how Stalin treats Santa just before the Russian Revolution forty-one years from now. He won't know about Sinterklaas, Krampus, or any other iteration of The *real* Santa™ either.

He won't know how that bastard The *real* Santa™ came to town or why he turned his thirteen children into greedy little birds, squawking for more stuff: Coca-Cola®, boots, books — yes, books — guns, licorice sticks, oranges, and gewgaws of all sorts. Gramps could know it, but he simply doesn't care. (Cos filling his head with settler nonsense doesn't help him raise sheep better, or develop a stouter strain of common wheat, one he can plant earlier, harvest earlier, replant and harvest again before winter sets in.)

So Gramps only thinks he hates The *real* Santa™: cos of the way he ruined his thirteen kids and cos he caught Granny Lanny, erm, kissing him in that special way. But really, the kids turned out okay — pretty much — and that kiss pales in comparison to the shenanigans Granny Lanny and Ziff got up to, hey? And he never stopped loving his kids and wife, did he? And it never even occurred to him to put a hate on his twin brother Ziff, right? And really, The *real* Santa™ was just another settler pulling settler shenanigans. So how does The *real* Santa™ garner so much bilious wrath?

Well, that hate in Gramps' guts was a third twin brother — triplet, I guess — who grew into a full-fledged inner child in his gut — let's call that third twin Frank — with its own agenda; Frank just wanted Gramps diverted so it could complete its own nefarious tasks. Them tasks include ending the world as we know it.

And do you think Gramps would let Frank carry out its evil schemes if he knew of them?

Yeah I married the old fart cos my mom said he'd make a good
match: good head for business, strong backed, potent sperm —
how she knew that, you ask? — she said she could smell it on
him, said he could knock you up with a look. I say, A look?
Silly superstition, Mum. Well, she said, he's put a baby in you
already. Naaaaaaaaaaaaah. Not a chance. I haven't said more'n
three words to him in like forever. You listening to me, my girl?
I said he could put a baby in you with a look. I didn't say
anything about putting babies in you with just words. Did I?
No, Mum. But I don't feel pregnant. You been pregnant before?
No. Then how you know what pregnancy feels like, hey? To
this point I only let certain boys touch my tits from outside,
and only Ziff has petted my pussy, also from outside my dress.
Ziff wants me to touch his spaeks?, wants me to suck it too.
I tell him, every time, I will when I'm ready. I will when it
feels right to me. He says he likes me a lot and he will wait.
He's said that to Isabel Black. He's said that to Constance Brown.
He's said that to Marie Arnold. We think he's said that to every
girl in town. Not one's ever said they've touched it or anything
else. No one's said Ziff's their first (or second or . . .). Thing is,
he may whore around, promising every girl he will wait until
they're ready to go. And I love him so much. Crazy-stupid-love.
If I could sneak out the house in a pants and shirt, I would let
Ziff do me and do everything he's asked me to. That's the thing
about Ziff, other boys beg and whine and try touching you no
matter how hard you swat their hands away, no matter how
hard you sock them in the jaw, not Ziff though. Ziff asks can
I touch you up top? And waits for you to answer. Yes: he takes

your boob soft and gentle, squeezes pleasure into you. His touch
sends shockwaves right to your pussy. Them other boys grab
at you like they want to pull your tit off. Gramps, like his twin
Ziff — they can't be identical because Gramps is more handsome
when you get right down to it — asks if he might hold your hand,
if he might kiss your cheek. Gramps hasn't once asked for any
of my sex. He wears his love for me so plain on his face. Cinchy
Gramps. Polite Gramps. Too easy. Too safe. Too boring, no
matter how potent his sperm. But ever nice to look at. Maybe if
he had his twin's lust, his twin's skilled hands. But naaaaaaaah.
Ziff, all crooked smiled, all gangly stoop, all magic hands, and o
my god, so fuckable. Anyways, Ziff and I and a bunch of us from
school picnic up kʷəlkʷléwt. Isabel and Constance and Marie
help Ziff and me sneak off. Today I will touch his spaeksʔ, but
not put my mouth on it. Soon as I get him behind that deadfall,
I yank him by the belt. Unbutton his fly. Take it out, I say. What?
he says. Take your damn cock out before I change my mind. O,
he says, and so cool, almost too slow for me, he flops it out. It's
not the first one I ever saw, mostly my brothers', but not in a bad
way. And there was that one time Jonathan McQuarry whipped
out his hard one and tried rubbing it on me. No way I would
run away from him. Who knows what he'd do if I turn my back
on him. My daddy showed me what to do when idiot boys try
these shenanigans on me. Jonathan McQuarry chants, suck-me-
fuck-me you lovely little squaw, you sweet-bottomed tease, you're
mine, you belong to me. I hike my skirts up a bit and say, As if.
Up comes my knee. Down goes Jonathan McQuarry, rolling
around the ground, both hands wrapped around his bits.

For a second or two I want to punt his sack into oblivion. But
Daddy says you have to be careful how you deal with səmséme?,
one wrong look and they will hang you. One wrong look and
they'll send you to jail. Ziff smiles his crooked smile. Let me
get comfor'ble, 'k? Jonathan McQuarry's throbbed and stood
just about straight up. Ziff's lolls outside his zipper like a dog's
tongue. And kind of ugly, all veiny — like Jonathan McQuarry's —
and hooded, not at all like Jonathan McQuarry's purple mush-
room-capped thing. Good god, it's broken or deformed! I say,
Now what? Ziff wriggles his pants partway down his thighs —
ever muscled, them thighs — bare arse on a bed of twigs and
what not. He says, Spit on your hands. Sick! No. No. No, he says.
You gotta touch it with wet hands, or you'll just give it a Indian
rope burn. On your spaeks?? Yeah, and it hurts way more than
on the arm. Way, way more. So spit, hey? I make a mouthful of
spit. *Ptui!* Like I have a mouthful of chew. Soon enough Ziff's
spaeks? looks like Jonathan McQuarry's, just darker, but no prettier. And three gobs of spit later Ziff moans, groans, grumbles,
and swats my hand away. No spit on his hand, but he cranks
on it like a steam piston. *Chuff. Chuff. Chuff.* Through clenched
teeth and hard breaths, he says, Put your mouth on it now. Put
your own mouth on it. Jeez you. I said I would when I'm ready.
Did I tell you I'm ready? And real grumpy, he spurts, Fine then.
His hand's a blur. Yes, he groans. He grumbles, yes. He moans,
yes. Back arched, hips thrust the air (Is this what fuck the world
looks like?). He croons, o-o-o-o-o-o-o-o-o-o-o-o-o-o-o-o-o-o-o-
o-o-o-o-o-o-o-o-o-o-o-o O-O-O-O-O ahhhhhhhhhhhhhhh,
and a cloud of smoke or dust plumes over his wickedly dancing

spaeks?. Looks like Indian paintbrush caught in a dust devil.
Homely thing, that cock. Maybe you should've spat on it, hey?
Your mouth on it would've worked better. As if.

This chapter reads a lot like Genesis 5, so go ahead and skip to the next one, if you wish.

Damn, you caught me in another lie. This chapter just tells all about all thirteen of Gramps and Granny Lanny's children.

Now you could say eighteen-year-old Gramps and sixteen-year-old Granny Lanny married cos of their first kid — you remember that one that doesn't feel like a pregnancy to Granny Lanny, way back in 1858? You could say that, but what if the Universe has a plan for them? What if that first child only serves as a device to movie this story forward? That would kinda cheapen the story, i'nit? I could pretend to know what the Universe or xeʔɬkʷúpiʔ have omniscient minds. But that's a priest's job, i'nit? That's a charlatan's job, i'nit?

The truth of the matter is both Gramps and Granny Lanny lived in youth's blissful ignorance. You make blissfully ignorant mistakes and you learn from them. And grow from them. Well, that's the general idea. So Gramps learned to look away when his lust simmered in his loins. And Granny Lanny started listening to her mother and her yéyeʔ, I mean really listen.

And they called that son of theirs Bliss. And Bliss lived at home his entire life. He didn't take a wife, a lover, a concubine. None a that. He sat in the attic and wrote poems and didn't eat and didn't sleep. At age forty-eight, he wrote himself into a rhyming couplet and that was that. Poof. Gone.

So them two, Gramps and Granny Lanny, think they make lousy parents and flawed children. Like their Bliss was somehow wrong. And they cry for him. And they read his poems. But them poems don't speak to them two, Gramps and Granny Lanny.

Okay, so sixty-seven-year-old Gramps and sixty-five-year-old Granny Lanny have their next twelve children between 1907 and 1937:

1907 — Twins, George and Georgia

George, cursed with the gifts of both his father and Uncle Ziff, has six children with six different girls and women by his twenty-first birthday. His rakish life shotguns to an end, a 12-gauge belly shot, nine days before his twenty-second birthday. An irate father who wishes he could shove the baby George puts in his seventeen-year-old daughter up George's arse. George's progeny inherits his potency, so Gramps and Granny Lanny have traced nearly a thousand grand-, great-grand, great-great-grand, and great-great-great-great-grandchildren. And Gramps and Granny Lanny comb Ancestry for their children's children's children's children's children, and each new child fills them with joy and sorrow. Sometimes more joy. Sometimes more sorrow.

Georgia shares her mother's pragmatism, and her father's melancholy. She lives to 104 and welcomes death. She too has outlived her five children and their father, who dies landing on Normandy beach. Georgia refuses to remarry or date after her husband's "heroic" end. Heroic cannon fodder for the damned Brits. Each generation of Georgia's line protests war: some become lawyers, and each of them fights for Indian and women's rights and re-instating the Indian status of Gramps and everyone else Canada's tricked out of theirs. With some success, but the puzzle they have yet to solve: Why do we need a damn card to prove our Indianness? A good question that, and you know it is because Canada has no answer, but sings an award-winning version of "The Sidestep." And to save you another trip to that great oracle the Google®: "The Sidestep," Dolly Parton ©1982, from the original soundtrack of *The Best Little Whorehouse in Texas*. Ghaaaa! Does that seem as cumbersome and pull-you-from-the-story to you as it does to me? Fuck aged pop cultural references, hey? As we're already off topic, I highly recommend watching the movie. It's a little racy, but Parton owns every scene in which she appears, and her version of "I Will Always Love You" is the best ever. *The best.* And she wrote it.

1909-1944, Guy and 1909-1982, Gal

After having back-to-back sets of twins, Granny Lanny says she will never have another baby. If they allowed elective hysterectomies, she would have one as soon as she heals from the twins' birth. Now Guy and Gal, each born two-spirited, and each spends their life in and out of jail for the crime of being themselves. Gramps and Granny Lanny encourage Guy and Gal to be themselves, but carefully. May as well ask them to switch shells. So, Gramps and Granny Lanny have one of their few fights over naming the twins. Guess who wins.

Gramps says, "Well you can name a boy Guy, so you can name a girl Gal."

"Cannot!"

"Why the hell not? No one's ever done it. Our daughter should be the first."

"And the last, no doubt."

"This one's important to me."

And Granny Lanny huffed. Settled into an attack stance and said, "So important you risk my eternal anger and our baby's lifelong ribbing over her name?"

"As far as I'm concerned, it won't be a problem for me or for Gal. Gal has other stuff to contend with. And you will find something else to be mad about soon enough."

"Sometimes your logic frightens me, old man."

"My resilience must scare you too, i'nit?"

"Naaaaaaaah! I like having you around. Kinda wish you'd spend more time here, but."

And Gramps eye-rolled, "Sure you do."

Sometimes I just want to slap Gramps upside his thick head. He's so observant in other ways, but can't see Granny Lanny past her ongoing affair with his brother, and especially not her indiscretion with The *real* Santa™. I'd rather he forget all about it, truly forgive Granny Lanny, but he insists he needs to hold onto the grudge to continue living. And maybe it's all part of that third twin's master plan. And The *real* Santa™ thinks Gramps will end his eternal life. As the chronicler of their stories I can, with a certain amount of confidence, state that they're both wrong.

And right.

But back to Guy and Gal. They rent a house together in Vancouver. They work opposing shifts at the Rogers Sugar plant. They have few friends. The Vancouver cops prey on them. Purportedly straight men prey on them. They find Guy floating near Siwash Rock. Despite his cracked skull; four broken ribs; subdural hematomas about the face, neck and chest; a combat

boot heel bruise on his left cheek, and another featuring the
whole sole on his solar plexus; the variety of objects they pulled
from his butt, including a half-empty bottle of JD; they ruled
his official cause of death an accidental drowning, even though
Guy had no alcohol in his system and no water in his lungs.
But Guy never took to alcohol cos he didn't believe booze helped
deal with life in any way whatsoever, just complicated already
complex problems.

Granny Lanny finds the three cops who kill Guy — Vancouver's
finest — Constables Evan Snow and Taylor Tracey, and Lieutenant
Robert "Never Call Me Bob" Westwood. Each of them dies of a
mysterious illness at the tail end of the polio epidemic. But polio
doesn't do them in. They don't fall to magical deaths. And they
don't drop dead from death curses. Them three stellar cops croak
in a slow painful cluster of illness marked by fever, extreme aches
and pains, abdominal cramping, vomiting, diarrhea, and weird
haemorrhaging, and bruising. Granny Lanny says, "I guess they
ate shit and died. Serves 'em right, hey?"

Gramps fumes silently. His nuclear rage could raze the city
and burn everyone in it. His answer to each wrong done to his
children and their children, et cetera, involves both barrels of
his 12-gauge. Granny Lanny disapproves, and, for the most part,
so do I. So Gramps fumes silently, swallows his cancerous rage,
nurturing that third twin, Frank.

Gal dies of food poisoning in a mental institution. She commits
herself to escape persecution at work and on the streets. Gramps
and Granny Lanny ask her to come home with them each time
they visit. And Gal, who by the way, absolutely loves her name,

says, "Kʷukʷscémxʷ, but you know I can't come home. They'll find me and they'll keep attacking till I'm dead, and they'll take you down too. And they won't care. And I can't do that to you guys. It's not right."

Neither Guy nor Gal have children.

1911–2003, Glenda

Gramps thinks, "O, yeah. We shall see about that. So long as I keep you pregnant, I keep you from messing with my brother."

You would think, with their children born under such chicanery, Gramps and Granny Lanny would despise them, and each other. But love.

The action kind of *love*. Not the word *love*. And Glenda is pure love. Heavenly love. But not naïve love and not blind love. She stays a virgin until she marries at twenty-four. She marries with a good man, who also embodies love. A good hunter who shares his catch with his parents, his in-laws, and as many old folks as he can. Sometimes he hunts just for them and he puts his net out for them two or three times a season, dries it, smokes it, and cans it for them. A good soldier with a knack for staying alive and avoiding incoming bullets and shrapnel. A hardworking man. They have nineteen children. Nineteen and not one set of twins, triplets, or quadruplets. Nineteen children! I do not have a vagina but it hurts just thinking about pushing out nineteen children. Glenda's entire line has highly proficient wombs. Their levels of good-heartedness varies. Gramps loves visiting Glenda's progeny. Granny Lanny cherishes them, but doesn't visit them while they walk the Earth.

She fears the jinx. That bad luck. She says, "Why mess with a good thing? And I can love them the same from over here as I can over there, with them squirming on my lap, and eating bannock with homemade strawberry jam, i'nit?" They know her as the nice old lady who sends them fifty dollars at Christmas and on their birthdays. Granny Lanny likes that they can send money and not sacrifice every meal for a month to pay for them gifts. She likes that part of wealth, the giving back.

1912–45, Glenn

Glenn stands alone among his siblings. Glenn alone could have been Ziff's, had Ziff any jism, even a few potent tadpoles ninjaing into Granny Lanny's uterus. And you just know Granny Lanny's eggs would've dropped their defences and greeted Ziff's with an honour guard and marching band. So complications from syphilis and HIV-induced pneumonia kill Glenn at thirty-three. I suppose it's a lucky thing that man-whoring Glenn up and dies without impregnating any girl or woman. And lucky for the women and girls that he doesn't infect them because he always asked if they would go if they knew he had deadly STDs. His parents taught him and the rest of his siblings to respect "no" in all its forms before it becomes "the thing" in like 2270.

"Saw you dancing out there. You got fine moves. Name's Glenn. Yours?"

"Not Glenn."

"Cool. Cool. I've got a sister named not Glenn."

"Do you?"

"Yeah. She's a coy one. Hard to get her to answer straight up at the best of times."

"You talk funny. Where you from?"

And Glenn says, "Nowhere. Sorry I wasted your time."

By this time, even if Glenn double-bagged it, he risked infecting her, so, he took his infected lust home with him, washed down a bottle of Lorazepam with LCB vodka and asphyxiated in his own vomit.

Before Tinder and them apps, guys and gals had to talk with each other. In person. And usually in super loud, super noisy bars and nightclubs. Lions have about a thirty percent success rate when they hunt, but even the studliest men and women maybe score less than five percent of the time — go by what you see and not what they tell you, okay? Cos they all lie.

But it was a great game.

And expensive. There was this one time, at The Roxy, I blew $356, including tip — a lotta money in them days, a whole week's pay — trying to snag this one woman, all spandex and big hair and lips and perfect little butt and six-inch heels and . . . ever wow, hey? So she laughs when I invite her back to my place. And she says, "O, honey, I'd love to, but my boyfriend's the jealous type . . ."

O, droop.

And don't let none of us old farts try telling you we chased after love back in them days, because we didn't. We thought maybe it could happen. Well, I know I wished it could. But the only women I ever snagged were rich white girls from the suburbs who slummed Indian bars hoping to snag themselves

some fine red meat. Seger, not Pete, but that other one, what's
his name?

Yeah, Bob. Bob Seger. Kʷukʷscémxʷ.

Anyways, that Bob Seger sings "Night Moves," that song
from the same-named album. And that's all it was. Knew a girl
once who called it mutual masturbation. Like double solitaire,
I guess.

And I guess once in a while we did care, or thought we did.

1915–2020, Garry

Garry. *Gar* as in gar and *y* as in ee. A typo on Garry's birth
certificate results in his name. They say it's a typo, but the typist
believes *Carry* is a typo and Granny Lanny and Gramps meant
Gary. She leaves the extra *r* because she likes the letter, and the
way it sounds when it rolls off the right tongue. She hasn't seen
Gramps or Granny Lanny talk much, if at all, so she has no idea
what a rolling *r* might sound like, but she can tell by the look
of them two that they're wrong-tongued. Granny Lanny has a
lifelong mad (maddening) crush on Cary Grant, born Archibald
Leach in 1905. Like (almost) everyone else on the planet, she's
old enough to be his father. Call her a cougar and she answers,
"R-r-r-r-r-r-row." But how does just thinking about snagging
younger guys make you a cougar? I suppose them churchies
who tell you thinking about this or that is already a sin could.

Anyways, Garry lives a good long life, has three wives die of
ovarian cancer, and the last one didn't have the stamina to live
as long as him. So after she dies, he packs a backpack, takes his
yellow labs Bart and Spuʔum and hikes up into the mountains,

despite his surviving kids' protestations. He wanders the territory, surviving on rabbits, berries, mushrooms, and occasionally a squirrel. Winters, he builds a small sʔístkn and it has a doggie-door for Bart and Spuʔum. Every time Spuʔum farts the small fire glows like a flash gun going off. Sometimes them farts kill a little fire, blow it right out.

Garry tells them dogs stories. They like the ones where snkẏép pulls a fast one on other creatures, but not so much when they pull a fast one on him. And they ignore him when he works a hide, but when he debones a critter, they glom on to him till he tosses them a hunk of fat, and bones with meat on them. Sure, they'd prefer home with its wind-proof walls and roof, and central heating and air. Who wouldn't, hey? Well, Garry for one. His clothes hold smoke like whatever stinks in a dryer sheet, and to him that smoke smells sweeter.

After wandering the territory for twenty-four years, Garry returns to his house and finds it full. His youngest son, daughter-in-law and their children have moved in, put in new windows, resodded the yard, planted a vegetable garden, restored their mother's flower patch, painted the mother and stepmother's carved grave markers, and packed all of his stuff into a BigSteelBox®. Garry's entire life now lives inside precisely labeled cardboard boxes neatly stacked inside that rented locker. He says to the ghosts of Bart and Spuʔum, "Lookit, they moved us into a mausoleum, i'nit? Maybe after I rest up a bit I'll dig us a grave right smack dab in the middle of my four wives, hey? More wives than a cat has lives. Almost. Hahaha."

No sooner does his bony butt rest on the recently asphalted driveway than his spirit breaks away from its ragged frame to swim the air around the place one last time. His spirit, now free from gravity, zips skyward, burns through the atmosphere, embraces sky's cold blackness, finds its place within a cluster of four stars, transforming into the fifth to become that happy face emoji constellation that has astronomers around the world all gaga. Look how far we've evolved as peoples, hey? We've gone from naming stars Orion's Belt, Cassiopeia, and such, to The Happy Face Emoji, which hangs in the northeastern sky, and you can see it best in December through February, if you care to look.

1917–1932, Gretchen

This child. What a handful! Gramps names her after Gretchen Hoyt Corbett, who plays Beth Davenport of *The Rockford Files.* Gramps has a mad crush on Beth, but Beth is a TV character; Gretchen is a real woman.

Granny Lanny scoffs, "You can't crush on that Gretchen girl."

"Why not?"

"Because you don't even know her. You just see someone called Beth Davenport and you think you know the actress."

Gretchen Hoyt Corbett's birthdate is twenty-eight years away yet, but Gramps being Gramps, just can't wait.

"Anyways, Beth's a prettier name than Gretchen."

Sometimes Granny Lanny doesn't understand why she even bothers talking to her husband. "But that name belongs to the TV not the person."

Every now and then he tries to visit Gretchen wherever she stays. But mostly he hangs around her place when she stays in Portland, cos he can drive there in less than a day, and the idea of New York City scares him. He considers knocking on her door, a single red rose bud in one hand and a bottle of Prosecco in the other. But naaaaaaaah! What if his lusty thoughts shoot a baby into her through his sexy eye? What if she laughs in his face and slams the door on it? What if she has a pair of three-hundred-pound bodyguards who tear him to pieces and then feed him to a pack of ravenous attack dogs? What if he's been stalking the wrong house all this time and the little old white-haired lady answers the door and drops dead of fright when she sees his dark-skinned arse, or calls the cops cos she believes he's a home invader? What if real life Gretchen is nothing like TV Beth, and not at all pleasant? Naaaaaaaah!

And he even gets a job constructing sets and he hates it and he doesn't bump into Gretchen/Beth even once. In 1977, he lands a non-speaking part as an extra, a Vietnamese refugee, in an episode called "New Life, Old Dragons."

The sweet young woman with the clipboard looks at Gramps and says, "Gramps is such an unusual name. How did that come about?"

Gramps thinks he should answer in his best Peter O'Toole impersonation, maybe his best Chief Dan George? Maybe Adam Beach from his days on *Law and Order: SVU*? Of course the kind young lady with the clipboard wouldn't know of Adam Beach, who's just five years old now and won't play Detective Chester Lake for thirty years, or *Law and Order: SVU,* whose first episode doesn't air for twenty-two years, so he smiles, and says in his best Vietnamese voice (pretty much his rez voice, cos he has no idea what a Vietnamese accent sounds like), "Kʷukʷscémxʷ. It was my grandfather's name."

In her sincerest eyerolling tone, Ms. Clipboard says, "Awwwwwwwww, how sweet. Listen, you play a Vietnamese refugee. No speaking. No looking into the camera. We pay you twenty-five dollars and provide a buffet lunch."

The buffet lacks chocolate dipped strawberries, chocolate fountains, champagne fountains, caviar, raw oysters, smoked oysters — oysters of any kind, really — beef Wellington, salmon Wellington, or anything else from the Wellington family — did they not get the invitation? — no pigs in blankets, no baron of beef, hell, not even a squire of beef either, no huge Virginia smoked ham, no fancy-schmancy roast turkey, turducken, although Chef Paul Prudhomme serves it up at his restaurant — not many people outside of New Orleans know it exists yet — no pheasant under glass, above glass, or wearing glasses, no fancy salads with croutons, sprinkled with crisp bacon crumbles, no finger sandwiches, no beef tongue sandwiches (kʷukʷscémxʷ, xeʔɬkʷúpiʔ), no fresh baked rolls and buns, and on the dessert table, not a single brownie, carrot cake, bundt cake, coffee cake, no cake of any kind, no petit fours or fives or sixes, no fine Belgian chocolates (in 1977 even the most socially conscious people do not know about fair trade and slave-free chocolate), no baked Alaska, no Pavlova with fresh strawberries and pine-apple, and no Pavlova with frozen fruit and canned pineapple chunks either.

Okay, that's a long way of saying they got one of them giant sub sandwiches, on white bread, and some rusty grapes, and a few stuffed green olives. Some feast, hey?

So after a hard day of waiting to shoot his scene, playing a Vietnamese refugee herded from one tiny encampment to another, then loaded onto a boat and sent across the ocean to a land that doesn't belong to him. Aside from the playing a Vietnamese refugee, Gramps doesn't feel like the role is too much of a stretch for him. He takes a chunk of that soggy sixteen-foot submarine sandwich, a lukewarm tin of Tab® (because Granny Lanny says he can only drink diet soda or water, and he will not drink the water in LA), and a butter-scotch Jell-O® pudding. They put out plastic knives and forks and spoons, because they will not think of the spork (although the spork is around since the nineteenth century, no one really knows about it until much, much later — see, I can use the Google® too) until they start to worry about all the plastic waste we feed to birds, herptiles, and marine life.

So the story about how Gretchen got her name has no bearing on her short life. But Gramps likes to tell it, and I tell it with his permission. Just the same, Chuckie says he tells it better than me. Maybe he does, but you're stuck with my telling until he comes along to tell it to you in his way.

Yeah, so Gretchen lives fifteen adventurous years. She wishes she can fly like Amelia Earhart, and she would finagle her way onto her heroine's last flight, had she not kicked the bucket five years prior to its launch. What do you do when freakishly powerful winds swirl you up inside a dust devil and deposits

you like a sackful of kittens into River? Try telling Gretchen
to stay home. Try telling her not to race into town to catch the
freak show passing through (I have never noticed the pun in
this hoary old phrase before. Noice!).

1918-2007, Grace

Anything but graceful, Grace shows none of the skills of the
dancer she dreams as her life's calling. Her dreams have her
in a tutu, starring in The National Ballet of Canada which
will form in Grace's thirty-third year, and after she's aged out
of the competition for a place in the company. She could have
chosen to grow up a jingle dress dancer, a new dance catching
fire throughout Ontario's Indian Country (yes, Wisconsin and
Minnesota, too), but she still has no rhythm, can't find the beat,
can't follow her teacher's instructions, and she can't sew her
own regalia, no matter how much she concentrates.

But Grace can draw. Before her second birthday she draws a
ballerina in a graceful leap across the stage. The chiaroscuro of
green poop on white walls stuns you with its beauty as it chokes
you with its odour. When Grace hears this story throughout her
life, she doesn't hear the beauty part, just the paints walls with
her poop part.

Eventually she modifies her dream from dancing to captur-
ing dancers' grace on canvas and tintypes and Palladiotypes
and gelatin dry plates and giclee. Some of her older paintings
and photos hang in the Indigenous Art Gallery and galleries
around the world. She receives the Order of Canada for her
service to Indigenous arts in 2006. Her family, with the band's

blessing and support, converts her home into a museum, where you can view her Order of Canada pin, her darkroom, her paint studio, her computer studio, where she made 3D sculptures, short animated films, her foley and sound studios. Good thing she has five children and each has their own room. Good thing she actually makes enough as an artist to convert her home into a creative studio.

She invents the concept of poor lip synching, not for its accidental humour, but because her lack of rhythm poisons her sound work too. She doesn't notice, or pretends not too. No one knows. You can see some of her animated shorts on the National Film Board website. In her own way, she too has achieved near-eternal life.

1919–1939, Gabe

Gabe bursts from Granny Lanny's womb like a cop kicking in your bedroom door. He speaks to his mom in dreams, and from the moment he can swim, that little tadpole rams the walls of his cage, looking for a way out.

"Don't even think about calling me Gabriel, Mum. I'm no angel."

"No," says Granny Lanny, "I see your point."

Gabe chomps the umbilical cord, wrenching it like a dog on a perp's ankle. The tighter he clamps down the woozier he gets and his resolve to not evacuate the amniotic fluid's zero gravity haven collapses. *Real men, even tadpoles like me, don't live soft, smothering lives.* Granny Lanny winces, waking Gramps. Gabe releases the umbilical. "And don't you forget it, Mum."

"Jeez you! How could I?"

"You sleep talking, Lanny-Panny, or talking with the tadpole again?"

"A bit of both, my husband. A bit of both."

"What's he up to tonight?"

"O, just reminding me about his name."

"How bout we just call him Boy. Works for that Tarzan fellow."

"I let you have Gal. No way you get *Boy* or any other goofy name."

"I am the husband, so my word's the last word."

"As if."

"Hahaha."

She punches his arm.

"I love you too, Lanny-Panny."

"Ach, you, don't get all mooshy on me now. Go to sleep."

"I'm already halfway there. Tell the tadpole goodnight for me."

"He says, 'Tell me yourself, you senile old fart.'"

"Hmmm, then Gabe, it is. I guess. That tadpole's got some fierce attitude."

They laugh. Gabe fumes. *You want attitude? I'll give you attitude.*

He does. Funny thing, though. You'd think he'd be a bully and all sorts of toxic male things. But no. Stubborn, for sure, but mean only to his parents. The kid you see at home differs so much from the kid you see at school.

"Which one's our son, Lanny-Panny?"

"Both. But I sure could do with a little less of the devil boy."

Hahaha.

Gabe wants the sea, to breathe its moist air, to sail on it, to hunt whales (you can hunt whales legally in them days), to catch black marlin, and bluefin tuna, and spring salmon (chinook, tyee, king). As soon as he turns seventeen, he hitches a ride to Halifax. He smells adventure. He smells conflict. Three weeks after leaving the plateau he accepts a gig as a deckhand on the ss *Athenia*. Hard work. Little adventure. Little pay. But Gabe finds home at sea in his bunk below the waterline. And on 3 September 1939, he gets his first and last taste of battle. Gabe, asleep and trapped below the waterline, kicks the hatch latch till he runs out of kicks, one of 117 casualties as the Germans sink the *Athenia*, just as they do in 1917. After that first German torpedo incident, you would think the owners would leave the name *Athenia* at the bottom of the Atlantic.

Mom, I'm real sorry. Tell Pops goodnight for me.

She winks. "Tell him yourself."

1921–1986, Gavin

Gavin's status card arrives in February 1986. Gavin expires five years before the card. Another win for Canada. And still, Gavin smiles, giddy as Scrooge on Christmas morning.

"Since when do you need a card to know you're an Indian?"

"O, Ma, I don't need the card to know who and what I am. Having it just makes it so the government has to treat me with dignity and respect."

Shaking her head, Granny Lanny says, "My son, all I ask is don't hold your breath. Got it?"

"Why don't you and Dad go for yours. It's about time you get recognized for who you are. And they've robbed you all these years."

"That card won't stop them robbing us."

"Still, you're getting up there, and if you get your cards you can retire in comfort."

"I got a lotta years left in me, my son."

Gavin, as you may have guessed already, lives with a this-cup-is-full-or-will-be-any-moment-now kind of guy. He hunts, fishes, fights, and works as hard as anyone. If he goes out for a moose, he will come back with a moose. He will butcher his catch. He will tan the hide. His sausages, a little too spicy for Gramps — who eats them anyways — stay melt-in-your-mouth moist, and just greasy enough to make them decadent.

Gramps, after eating too many of Gavin's sausages, Dutch ovens Granny Lanny. He laughs while she flops around like a net-snagged sockeye. When he frees her from his oven, he catches a whiff of his own stink. He turns green and runs from the room, just as he does while changing diapers. After some 500,000 poopy diapers, you'd think Gramps might have learned a trick or two about overcoming the stink or developed a tolerance to it. But no.

Gramps escapes the bed before Granny Lanny's fist finds his face. He drives all the way to Vancouver and buys four dozen long-stemmed roses. He doesn't understand how textured paper has any real value. A bushel of beets has real value. A stack of tanned hides has real value. A hind quarter of moose has real value. Hell, quarters of all larger game animals have value.

Back home he would trade a box of canned fish for the roses, but she's sold out at the moment. He could have driven to The Loops and been home faster, but he likes to marvel at the spectacle of lights on Granville Street's theatre row — not so much nowadays, but in the early-'70s, before they decide to pack a hundred screens into a single building you can choose a family show at the Vogue, or sneak into one of the porno theatres on the west side of the street. And the people out at night. Holy! Everyone in town must want to go to catch a film (or eat a meal, or party, or shop, or something else).

The florist can only fit one dozen red roses into a single box. Gramps carries out four of them. He lays out his good tarp and packs the roses carefully onto it and surrounds them with blocks of ice and heads toward home.

He gets to Richmond instead and it baffles him. He checks his map. He points his car east, follows loops and spirals, crosses bridges, and lands at YVR. Three times he drives in circles.

He knows he's made another circle when he passes the airport parking sign.

"Hahaha, just relax, old timer. We'll get home before the ice melts yet."

He relaxes and soon he turns onto South East Marine Drive, and not long after that onto the Trans-Canada East.

Granny Lanny has plenty of time to burn off her anger. She chooses to hold a little of it, just a dash, to spice up Gramps' homecoming. "The least I can do for that old bastard, i'nit?"

Arms laden with roses, Gramps knocks on the door with his knee. Granny Lanny doesn't know the knock, but she knows it's Gramps at the door. Even though she doesn't know why he knocks instead of coming in like he owns the place, she takes her sweet time. Passive-aggressive act begets passive-aggressive act.

In a perfect world Gramps stands at the door loaded down with a two-hundred-pound package in his arms, straining his puny arms and rubber-boned back. But the world's far from perfect; Gramps, a wiry old fart, could still drive rail spikes like penny nails, if they still needed people to drive them by hand. He can still fall an eighty-foot pine tree with a hand axe, but prefers to use his chainsaw, a tool so old it's forgotten its name, and so has he.

So Granny Lanny, armed with angry eyes and poison arrow words, yanks open the door. She doesn't think Gramps will come home drunk because he never has. She doesn't think he runs out on her to buy her a new fridge because he does that the year before. And she doesn't think he'll bring home a smart TV because he does that in two years and she makes him take it right back. Despite the fact that it will talk with you and find your favourite shows, and if it listens, who knows who's listening at the other end. "What?"

Gramps' bowed legs and shaggy silver and black hair and lumberjack hands. Gramps' goofy smile. Four long, brown paper boxes. And says, "I kept it iced, so it should be okay."

The dollop of anger she's reserved to fuel her attack melts like a summer ice cream cone. Well, not quite, because it doesn't ooze onto her hand and make a sticky mess and water-log the cone. Now, as in many thousands of other moments, she understands why she has stayed with Gramps all these years. "I don't know how you do it, old man, but you never fail to surprise."

One dozen long-stemmed red roses has the romantic flare of Brad Pitt wooing Angelina Jolie, where you are one of them two. Four dozen long-stemmed red roses, by my reckoning, is overkill. Who even has a single vase large enough to hold them with their greens and baby's breaths? Granny Lanny doesn't, and that's for sure. And even arranged in the old blue enamel canner, them roses' magnificence glows.

But their glorious aroma fails to mask the memory of Gramps' sausage-fart smell.

So Gavin's story leaves Gavin mostly out of it. Gavin prefers it this way. His cup-full view of life also marks humility so pure that he appears invisible to most people.

Of all their children, Gramps misses Gavin most.

1925–2003, Gwendolyn

In her later years, Gwendolyn fancies herself regal, a princess like Jasmine, like Ariel, like Belle, like Pocahontas. She watches them Disney® DVDs with her grandchildren, then some of her great-grandchildren. She takes her children to see *Pinocchio, Cinderella, Alice in Wonderland, Pinocchio in Outer Space,* and even live-action films, a lot of westerns. She grows up thinking Indians are evil. She grows up believing that Indians are bad, Indians are lazy, and Indians are a bunch of drunken louts. She and her family live off rez, so they are white, maybe a little more tanned than most of them other white people, but white nonetheless.

Before losing herself in westerns and Disney® films, Gwendolyn reads the Arthurian romances, the adventures of Charlemagne and the Three Musketeers, Trixie Belden, though a little old for that series of books. She understands the love affair between Lancelot and Guinevere, and knows that a love like theirs is the only love good enough for her.

The day after she turns twenty-one she packs her bags and moves to Vancouver to go to secretarial school and get a job in the steno pool of a company to find her Lancelot among its executives.

After five false starts and a child from each, she finds a sort of Lancelot. He adapts to her past and children, each bearing their father's surnames (again, to save you from calling on the mighty Google®: *last names* were once called *surnames*). She has two more kids with her late-arriving prince. She tells him that her family dies in a fire after a car crashes into the house. He believes her. Her children believe her. Her parents find her anyway. Their grandparents find them anyway. Gwendolyn's true Lancelot does not.

She lets her children visit the grandparents. The children already share six sets of grandparents between them, so adding another pair to the bunch doesn't change things very much at all. The three older grandchildren embrace the hippy movement and dress like their noble-savage-inspired peers.

Gramps shows them how to make (most of you young whipper snappers will say *craft*) medicine bags and pipe pouches.

"No. We don't use bone breastplates or quill chokers. And no beaded headbands, wristbands, and such. And don't even talk to me about dreamcatchers."

One of them takes the brown acid at Woodstock and tries to outrun a speeding locomotive.

One of them gets shot by the FBI at Wounded Knee.

One of them makes billions after designing a line of runners favoured by everyone who jumps onto the running and jogging fashion fad of the '70s.

Ach! Someone walking over my grave again. I got some witch's cold breath chilling my neck. Naaaaaaaah! It's your boyfriend that Santa. That *real* Santa™. We got nothing going on. Seen you two going at it. Screwing like them humpingback whales. In my house. While your kids sleep. We didn't screw, old man. I just sucked his dick. Same difference. As if. I just wanted to thank him for all those great presents he brought. Everyone else in the world leaves out cookies and milk. We had none. No flour. No baking powder. No vanilla. No chocolate chips. We'd eaten our last two boxes of KD®. No turkey. No ham. No potatoes. No rice. No canned peas. Nothing. Again. Not my fault. Nothing ever is, i'nit? Hey, where you think you're going? To Ansel's. Course you'd rather hang with your damn friends than spend any time with me. Not even. Then why you walking out on me again. Off he goes. Such a waste of good tears. Such a waste of years. I wish he'd yell. I wish he'd slam the door. Punch a wall. Anything that shows he has feelings. One brother leaves out the front door, the other sneaks in the back. Closing the door with barely a click. Tiptoeing through the kitchen. I know who's there. Just get your butt in here, fool. Damn girl, you got some good radar on you, i'nit? I could hear them clown-shoe feet of yours coming a mile away. Clown feet? You know what they say about men with big feet. I know. And it's a lie. He laughs. So the husband ran off to Ansel's again? Tight-lipped nod. Just half a sigh. You know what goes on there? I hear rumours, but haven't seen it myself. Who'm I kidding? I know as good as Ziff here what those pervy men do there. Better my husband comes in a bucket there than anywhere near me.

You like me better. Why not just leave him to his gambling and shit? Sometimes I wish I could. Whether love or old habit, I can't kick him out and I can't walk out the door myself. You say that like you want to stay a prisoner in your shit marriage. He gives me thirteen babies. And I give you nothing but sex that leaves you hogtied with rapture. O, and that dust. That doesn't count for anything, i'nit? It keeps me from going insane from boredom. So let's get to work on that boredom problem of yours. Ever the romantic, you. Ziff and I don't do our sexing in front of an audience. So give us our privacy and just flip the page, okay? Well Ziff would. Such a show-off, that guy. But not me, so hurry up and flip the damned page.

First off, let me tell you I do not now nor have I ever lived at the North Pole and not the South Pole, either. I have a private island about three hundred miles north of Fiji. If Gramps ever figures out he won't ever find me at the North Pole, I'm one dead Jolly Old Elf™. One thing the stories get right, maybe the only thing, is that elves once crafted — as they like to say nowadays — toys for all the boys and girls. The naughty list is pure bullshit, piled onto a bunch of old bullshit stories. Let's face it, no little boy or girl is always naughty; okay, so I can name a bunch, but the mostly-good ones far outnumber them. Even those hateful brats get something, and not a lump of coal. If I hear one more parent threaten their child with a lump of coal instead of the latest fad toy . . . Ghaaa!

Those empty threats render me speechless. Speaking of toys, the elves demanded a living wage. They seemed satisfied with our working relationship: they work, and I supply them with food and shelter and uniforms. My little helpers were satisfied and happy until 1 January 1863. Then the ungrateful bastards demanded land, living wages, and one day off each week.

"Or else," they threaten.

"Or else what? You little fucks have nothing without me."

"Give us what we want, or we won't make another toy, gewgaw, recorder, or ukulele. Nothing!"

"You strike and I will toss you out of your dormitories. Take back all the clothing I've supplied you. Take back all the cafeteria vouchers I've lavished on you. Leave your naked and sorry asses on the beach. You'll come back begging for the way things used to be. You'll come back begging for your old jobs back."

Those little bastards sit naked on the beach, about six hundred of them, for three months. Sitting on the beach and singing something about overcoming. They sing about overcoming while the Pinkertons I hire to resolve the standoff beat the living snot of each and every one of my elves. Fuck me, that strike hurts my bottom line. This is 1895, the first year with no gifts from me, The *real* Santa™.

And the missus comes down with suffragette fever in 1903. I love her anyway. That thing with me and Granny Lanny, also in 1903, is just a mistletoe moment run amok. But my eye started wandering, and I lusted for a good old-fashioned woman, one who appreciated the *obey* in the original wedding vows. She didn't walk the Earth and I doubt she ever only lived in some bible-thumper's dream of the ideal woman. So I gave up on finding the biblically obedient woman, and let that thing happen with Granny Lanny in Christmas, 1903. And my one indiscretion has haunted me ever since. Now another thing the stories have fucked up completely is about my ride. Reindeer could fly until 1722, but the air gets so bad that asthmatic deer kept falling from the skies. That song "It's Raining Men" starts out as the Scandinavian ballad "It's a Reindeer Rain." Don't get me wrong, I love the idea of a team of reindeer pulling my sleigh through the night. I love the names they have in those stories too. Especially Rudolph, his name has none of his cohort's poetry. His shiny, red nose, that blinking beacon of hope and love and dedication warms my calloused heart or some other Grinchy cliché. Granny Lanny also warms, and heals, my calloused heart. The memory of our brief encounter grows warmer with each recollection. That fire, if unleashed on the multiverse, would reduce it to irretrievable ashes.

How she gets under my skin baffles me. How she's stayed under it baffles me more. I see why Gramps jealously protects her, why he wants to hurt me; I know I would demand the same were Granny Lanny mine. But I have neither intention, nor inclination to mow Gramps' grass again. One day I'd like to put his vendetta behind us, talk it through over a glass or six of fine Kentucky bourbon. Even though we suffer the same curse-blessing of nearly eternal life, I don't want or need anyone penetrating my personal space, not since the missus falls prey to the Spanish flu pandemic of 1918. She survives the bubonic plague pandemic. She survives the white plague. Scarlet fever. Yellow fever. She survives the 1820 cholera pandemic. But the Spanish flu undoes her.

During my grieving period I cavort with some of the elven women. Before that time, aside from the missus — and that one indiscretion with Granny Lanny — I've cavorted with no one. I've not burdened the missus with a child. Nor, as far as I know, would I burden Granny Lanny with one. But these sweet elvish woman each give birth to one of my bastards.

And complications arise.

I stop cavorting because the complications make everyone involved somewhat miserable. Truth be told, sexual congress provides me no pleasure and no relief from the hollow the missus had filled inside me.

Complications: How do I love my children, and treat them as employees? How do I protect them from accusations of nepotism? How do I protect their mothers, now blackballed and labeled as whores?

My concubines and children ought to revile me as much as their peers. Perhaps more, because I have next to nothing to do with them, and no hand or say in the bastards' rearing. How do I convince my elves that I've had a change of attitude? How do I make up for my egregious behaviour in the last century? For conning them into joining me on this curs-ed paradise?

One-by-one the elves start to die. Four-hundred-year old elvish men and women drop off like old humans. With their bodies as sturdy as healthy teenagers, their faces only slightly hardened by age, they croak and I incinerate them.

One young elf, perhaps one of mine, takes my hand between hers and squeezes. "It'll be fine, The *real* Santa™. You wait and see. One day we'll all be together in the Great Mushroom Patch."

"And we'll all join hands and sing 'Koom-by-fucking-ya,' right?"

Far too often my sadness disguises itself as bitterly smart-assed anger.

Rather than run from me as the others do, she pulls my hand to her cheek and embraces me with her eyes. Her so familiar eyes. Who is your mother, girl? Do you know what kind of monster your father is?

"When someone you love passes, sadness is inevitable."

"Love?"

What kind of love manifests itself the way mine has?

"Of course you love us. Everyone talks about how you saved us by bringing us to this island."

"Everyone?"

She giggles.

"My mother says sometimes we can't see the obvious until someone shows it to us. Face it. Despite the lousy pay and stingy benefits, we stay. Most of us could make small fortunes working in China. Some of us could cash out our pensions and make a killing in the stock market."

"You could? Then why haven't you?"

"Silly man, we love you . . . Most of the time . . . You can be a right pain in the bottom sometimes, but you still have a giant, sensitive heart. We've all seen you tear up while watching the 1951 *A Christmas Carol*. We all know how important it is for you to keep your promises to all the children . . ."

The urge to take her in my arms and wrap her in a fatherly embrace comes on like a panic attack. "Enough, child. You speak nonsense!"

No, what I do, I do for the bottom line.

Profit is my god.

Love confounds profit.

Profit is my god.

Love destroys business plans.

Profit is my god.

The child wraps her arms around me as far as they reach.
Into my bloated belly, she says, "I love you, Daddy."

Profit is my god.

My body won't reject her.

Profit is my god.

My body won't reject her.

Profit is my god.

My body won't reject her.

Profit is my god.

My body won't reject her.

Profit is my god.

Profit is my god.

Profit. Is. My. God.

And my body refuses to shove her away.

We embrace. What the hell is wrong with me? Heaving like
a daytime television wife is not good for business. This moment
of weakness boosts their bargaining power. Addled brains
Henny Penny: They will own me at our next bargaining session
/ What bargaining session? / I've fired their asses and contract
out their labour.

And they've all died or moved on before their contract
expires. All of the bastards, even that little one who hugs me,

have buggered off. They'd become appendages of a different age once the robots took over the assembly lines. Since the late '90s I've contracted production to five Chinese factories. Five sweet contracts that include shipping.

I've taken a huge hit to my income since the Coca-Cola® polar bears have usurped my Christmas™ image. The residuals from every movie, including *Santa Claus Conquers the Martians,* keep me from cashing in my investments and keep me from selling my entire enterprise to Amazon®.

Amazon® has spent the last decade trying to buy me out. Amazon Prime® and its free delivery is supposed to wipe me out. Parents can wait and order up to two days before Christmas™ and spend far less than they spend at my shop. If I'd had the vision and cahones of Jeff Bezos, I'd be a trillionaire already, and most of my equity would be liquid. I could simply sell Christmas™ and spend the rest of my days walking nude along my beach, drinking fine Kentucky bourbon, talking to no one, seeing no one, and hearing no one. And the beard would go. The damned thing's more work than it's worth.

And you will bring Granny Lanny home.

Where the hell did that come from?

In addition to the craps and Texas Hold'em tables, Ansel has porn in his horse barn. No one using that barn talks to anyone about it. But like nearly every secret, everyone knows about it. Many boys and some girls sneak onto Ansel's land and try to watch that porn. Some say they see it through cracks in the hay stall floor. And some actually do. Ansel lets them watch because they will pay him a buck a minute after they're legal. They all do. Ansel vets and revets every single one of his clients weekly.

Desperate guys have a stink and a look to them, a little like fish gone off. He's closed in all its stalls, put some soundproofing up. Puts in big screen television sets and smart Blu-Ray players.

His customers can watch internet porn anytime, so he provides them the classics, you know, *The Devil in Miss Jones, Behind the Green Door, Candy Stripers, Debbie Does Dallas*. Ten copies of each and only six stalls but every night someone doesn't get the film they requested.

He puts in comfortable vinyl chairs. Puts in hand lotion and lube. Puts in tissues.

He charges a buck a minute. Only one person in the booth at a time, after some guy brings in a woman he says is his smʔém and they want to try out something new. Turns out he brings in a rent-a-wife for the night. And his real smʔém shows up and trashes the place. Beats the rent-a-wife almost to death. Chases her up the alley. Beats her with a rock the size of Ziff's fist. Somehow the rent-a-wife lives. The guy disappears and for the longest time we think his wife's buried him under her roses.

Ansel says later that she ought to have beaten her husband instead. She might have at that, because, as I said, no one ever sees him again. Mind you, no one really looks; no one asks after him. Funny how some people's names fade. I can sort of call up that smʔém and her husband's faces, their voices. But no names. Anyways, some cops raid Ansel's barn. Smash it up, steal his stash and put charges on him. He learns how to make a better porn barn in prison. So far, it works, that new plan. He knows who and what you are with a single sniff. Or two. Or three.

Accuracy counts.

Certainty counts.

He sniffs Gramps. His woes stink as sharp as balsamic vinegar. His horniness, with its note of cinnamon, barely registers. The horniest men smell like cinnamon and pickling spice. The horniest men vibrate as they hand over their cash deposits. Cash-only business now. No tabs. No cheques. No chickens. No booth sharing, as I've already said. Not Gramps though. So calm you want to check for a pulse. Every other man uses tissues. But Ansel hands Gramps a gallon pail. Gramps, pail in hand, chooses antique nudies. Nineteenth- and twentieth-century French postcards, naughty playing cards, the ones with nude Asian beauties, each with a lovely flower painted over her vagina; cheesecake; Vargas girls; Betty Page stills and shorts, and digital copies of *Exotique*.

Va-va-voom, hey?

Forty minutes of nostalgia and melancholy.

Forty minutes of passive strokes.

The short film of Betty Page in leather lingerie taking a cat-o'-nine-tails spanking on her fine white bottom engorges him. And true to form, a few seconds later, he gushes his load into the pail. Well mostly into the pail. Some splash-back and some dribbles splatter the floor, chair, and his shins.

He falls back into the chair, sticky with his sweat.

Long, slow breaths.

Just-fucked eyes glaze passively at the screen. Still Betty Page. He considers her change of heart about her work. He considers his nonsensical fascination with this specific clip. He wonders whether they share a connection. Each engaged in activities that do not please them. Would she hate him for desiring her short films to engorge him, and bring on the so-called happy ending? How happy can the ending be when it fills you with shame, with questions about your predilections?

What if you're a latent sadist, Gramps?

What if you're a latent masochist, Gramps, needing the pain of shame to get off?

Maybe none of the standard answers fit you, Gramps. Maybe you get a thrill from seeing that black whip swatting Betty Page's gleaming white bum.

Ansel's barn, surmises Gramps, allows me to go back in time without the pain of living those moments again. Face it, if Ansel's antique porn meant anything at all to you, Gramps, you could weave them live-shoots into your own timelines. (When Gramps talks to himself, he often refers to himself by name; it helps him keep track of the argument, as he alone defends all of its sides: Gramps, Me, Myself, and I. Too bad his mom didn't

give him middle names, hey?) He could bring Ansel mint copies
of them old dirty pictures and make a mint selling them to that
old perv Ansel.

But Gramps hasn't thought about it once. Although he has
wondered how Betty Page has remained a secret to so many
for so long. His curiosity ends here. He doesn't take the time
to look for word of her when he drifts back. His single focus
remains on finding that bearded Lothario, The *real* Santa™.

Christmas, 1903.

Remember that date, dear reader, Christmas, 1903.

Gramps goes back to that Christmas and relives all of its
pain. The pain of enfranchisement, his reward for earning the
1939–45 Star, the Canadian Volunteer Service Medal, the Dieppe
Bar. Some others. Thank you for your loyal and heroic service
Gramps; now you and your family are real Canadians and not
beggarly savages. Funny how Gramps, Granny Lanny, and
their thirteen children don't feel any less Indian and any more
Canadian. Instead of a house – of sorts – they stay at the Happy
Valley Inn, once a nineteenth-century luxury joint – in modern
parlance a resort – at the edge of town that has burnt up, three
times already: An arson fire in 1867, they say it rooms a bunch
of Pinkertons and scab labour, Chinamen and such; a kerosene
stove fire in 1922; and the Great Town Fire of 1923, a fire for
which they never find a cause, but rumours abound, and yet
another mystery Gramps might solve should it occur to him.

They stay at the Happy Valley Inn, not for its indoor plumbing, not for its hotplate, not for its mini fridge but because
it's the only place in town that rents rooms by the day/week/

month, and the only one that rents to Indians. Says so right on their sign. You just have to take a form to the Indian agent, and later on to white welfare instead, that lets it pay your rent off the top of your cheque. You just have to sign a paper that allows the Happy Valley Inn to not give you clean sheets and towels, and no toilet paper. But the children bring it home from school anyways.

Janitor Jim trades a sack of toilet tissue and paper towels for the girls' underpants. He trades a shopping bag full of tea, coffee, hot chocolate, and soup powder — all paid for by the school board — if they let him watch them take off their underpants.

Granny Lanny asks, "Why you keep losing your gonch at school, girls?"

They shrug and mumble, "I dunno, Mum."

Sometimes one of the younger girls says, "I had a accident in it, so I put it in the garbage, Mum."

But not too often, because Granny Lanny gets them in to the doctor so fast — to make sure their bladders don't have infections and that. Makes sure they have no inflammation on their shooshies, the word her Grade Three teacher taught her to say, because *vagina* is an ugly word, a vulgar word, a wash-your-mouth-out-with-soap word. Call her on it and she shrugs and says she doesn't make the rules, but follows them. Gramps wants his Grade Three daughters to call it *cunt* in class, then maybe *vagina* won't sound so vulgar, hey? And their Uncle Ziff promises five bucks to the one who says it first.

But when she says the c-word at home, he hunts his a-hole brother and tells him to stop corrupting his nieces. Ziff thinks teaching kids this kind of words in English or nɬeʔkepmxcín is funny as shit. And Gramps dislocates Ziff's jaw. And when your eight-year-old calls her vagina *pussy,* you laugh. You just can't help yourself. And when she calls it *pee pee,* you tease her — gently, but still you tease her.

But when she calls her vagina *shooshie,* you don't really know how to react; how can something so beautiful not have a name?

Granny Lanny's curiosity sends her up and down those years at the Happy Valley Inn. Unlike her husband, she loves visiting the days her children walk the sunny side of the planet. When she tells Gramps her babies live, he knows they do, but they die too, and most of them don't live to ripe old ages, not that they want their children curse-blessed with near-eternal life.

Neither can she uncurse their too-short ones.

Anyways, Granny Lanny says to Gramps, "Listen you, that janitor at the kids' school's messing with our girls."

Gramps loads the 12-gauge, then pulls on his boots. Granny Lanny snatches the gun away from Gramps. "No, we have to be smart about this. What good are you to us if they lock you up for life, or hang you, hey?"

"So what you propose we do about that janitor?"

Gramps himself has several, each starts with "kill him, then . . . ," or ends with ". . . then kill him."

Granny Lanny pulls tight her lips and leaves her body. Moments later, she returns and says, "Leave it to me."

Gramps seethes to their gardens. He pulls weeds. He dead-heads day lilies, basil, and cilantro. He waters the ground around the roots of the tomatoes, peppers, melons, cucumbers, potatoes, carrots, and beets. Dusk's chill slaps him back into the present by the time he has tended the vegetable patch. No small feat. That patch covers the better part of an acre.

Granny Lanny would never admit to her desire to simply kill that janitor. Nor does she believe the RCMP will help her daughters; she can't recall a single instance in her 181 years where they upheld the law for anyone she knew, knows, or will know.

She has a simple plan: Make him eat his own nuts, get him to sign a confession, and take his stash of girls' gonch, and pictures.

So.

Granny Lanny disappears for a day, a night, and another day.

She gets home all ragged, with big dark circles under her eyes and breath so bad it swaggers around her with razor wire wrapped around its fists.

She takes care of the janitor.

She upholds the girls' right to justice.

When they rebuild town, they install indoor plumbing in all of its homes and businesses. Most of the residents fight the addition of indoor plumbing. Sure, the convenience of drawing water from a tap inside interests many, but when it comes to voiding waste, most animals know better than to crap where they eat and sleep. The rez has no indoor plumbing. Enfranchisement and the promise of indoor plumbing, the right to vote and drink legally lured some away from the rez. Let's face it, a signature on a piece of paper and Social Insurance Number didn't actually strip away anyone's Indianness. How could the government take away something that xeʔɬkʷúpiʔ has privileged you? Only when some of your family says you sold your birthright to drink, that's when it sets in — you're unwelcome in town among the other səmsémeʔ because you're too dark and even with your SIN, too savage, and you're unwelcome back home because you've turned your back on your family, as either a drunk or Indian-hater in Indian skin, or an apple — Indian who thinks they're white.

Even Gramps, even though the Canadian government tricks him into white society, he and his family get shunned by some. Sure, good thing to go off and fight a war when they needed his help, but why fight for a country that ain't even yours? That war, and the deaths of his children, places in time he refuses to visit, suggest fate rules over free will. No matter what you manage to change, if you can. Those places hold omnipotent pain, deeper than that which follows his forty minutes with Betty Page and his other antique babes. Christmas, 1903, however painful, remains the one place he goes. He watches Granny Lanny and The *real* Santa™, impotent to change the moment, unable to

stop reliving it. Reliving that moment, he re-earns his goat
horns — he will find out for sure about Ziff and Granny Lanny
in 1967, the Summer of Love. Reliving that moment, however
painful, supports his theory that he is a masochist with control
problems. Gramps says newspapers and magazines have issues;
people have problems, challenges, or plain bad luck.

He visits a bondage sex toys online store. The prices scare
him, but a forty-three-dollar cat-o'-nine-tails might suit his
purposes. Not too cheap and not too dear, and made of real
leather: nice, if you like that sort of thing. Anyways, who can he
ask to spank his bottom? Granny Lanny might enjoy gagging
him. But flogging his tiny ass? Not likely. He considers driving
all the way to Vancouver to search out a leather bar, or brothel
with a woman who knows how to punish. Who enjoys punish-
ing. Who has the patience to teach a newbie the ropes.

Get it: the *ropes?* Aww, come on, that's brilliant wordplay.

No?

O, well.

Anyways, before spending a dime at Etsy®, Amazon®, or
Madam Erotíca's House of Leather and Vinyl, he tries it to see
if flogging his bare ass gives him true sexual release, that true
emotional orgasm they say some men enjoy.

Between taking revenge on The *real* Santa™ and living with
chronic depression, his sex drive is locked up in the mental
version of a Denver boot. So forget that emotional orgasm,
should it even exist, cos he can't even achieve plain old physical
release.

He has heard he can find The *real* Santa™ in Vancouver.

His source continues to dish up useful information, and refuses to take a payment, or tip.

Gramps knows anything free proves expensive in the end. But that snitch's information remains golden. So maybe they hate The *real* Santa™ as much as Gramps?

Could be. But . . .

The *real* Santa™ feeds information to Gramps' source. Often false information, but he occasionally sends accurate location data to Gramps, this time for instance, The *real* Santa™ has business in Vancouver. He could hold this meeting anywhere in the world, but he wants to check on his strip club and cam girl businesses. The *real* Santa™ wants to meet with Gramps. He wants to talk Gramps out of killing him. He wants to dazzle Gramps with brilliant words and superlative closing skills. It will cost him money and pride. Mostly pride. Hell, money comes and goes, and The *real* Santa™'s comes more than it goes.

Still, a gamble, but his immortality doesn't rely on strong emotions or adoration.

It could.

But naaaaaaaah.

If pleasure can haunt you, my brief encounter with Granny Lanny haunts me. A wordless encounter, Granny Lanny in charge every step of the way. No person, not even the missus has ever held me in thrall like Granny Lanny, and her power over me thrills and frightens me in equal measure.

Still.

The first time I meet Gramps, he runs at me with a venti full-party café mocha at the Robson Street Starbucks® (so much for my godlike negotiation and closing skills). The Starbucks® on the south side of the street, not the one opposite it. The south side store has an artsier ambience, and inspires me to compile my memoir as a screenplay. Black felt beret, or red, or dun.

No.

Just no.

The Navy surplus peacoat fends off Vancouver's November dampness, but suits me as much as a gold-filtered Capri® or rag-end Gauloises® tucked behind my ear. So the screensaver on my MacBook Pro® dances hypnotically across the screen. My flat white, now too cold to drink, and my inspired moment has passed and abandons the cursor in Scrivener®

waiting

waiting

forever waiting

on that single character that starts the magical flow of million-dollar words.

The Scrivener® cursor morse codes, "Just one word, one letter. An uppercase *I*, perhaps? Or start your screenplay with 'FADE IN.' Damn it, The *real* Santa™, I'm writing software, not a fucking writer; I can't write your story for you. Dammit all anyways, type something, The *real* Santa™. I can't have you giving me a bad name!"

At what point does my life begin? How does it end? What, if anything, makes my story worth reading or watching?

I ought to focus on Gramps' seething anger. And his rage, so fiery even its memory brings my flat white back to an undrinkable 190°F. It bubbles. And then splashes over the lip of the cup.

Gramps' attack silences the exuberant crowd of office tower people and wannabe writers who hope the same magic that bestows the Harry Potter® books to Rowling will give them a bestselling Harry Potter® clone, the next *Casablanca,* or the next *Fast & Furious* action blockbuster.

Gramps charges at me, slopping whipped topping and mocha onto his wrist. "You're a dead man, The *real* Santa™, or whatever you call yourself."

"I will die, perhaps. In time. But not today."

His mocha splats all over me. It scalds. It burns. He clocks me one in the jaw. It cracks, but doesn't hurt as much as the root canal I need afterwards, nor as much as the procedure to reset my jaw.

Everyone in the place has their phone up. Only the manager calls the cops. The rest post their videos of Gramps' attack on social media. Not one of their mostly-portrait-format videos goes viral. And not one of them makes the national, regional, or local news.

The cops show up pretty quick because Gramps' dark skin makes him seriously more evil. Sixty-three people, everyone in the store, save me and Gramps, fear for their lives. Okay, no one actually says the words *dark skin,* but they say they fear for their lives. (Beware the crazy Indian wielding a deadly café mocha; he'll kill us all! Never more. Never more.)

Four cop cars — eight cops — cavalry into Starbucks®, tasers drawn. At least eight customers call play-by-play while live-streaming this epic takedown.

I mumble, "Wait just one minute there, my children." Just try enunciating clearly with a broken jaw. "I have the situation well in hand. My friend and I have had a minor difference of opinion. I acted inappropriately and earned that shot in the mouth."

Santa's reputation as the vengeful gift giver and moral arbiter, the lord of naughty and nice, along with a little sleight of mind, stills the cops.

They often mistake me for a street person off his meds.

They often mistake me for a mall Santa.

They often mistake me for a Salvation Army Christmas Kettle Santa.

Only children seem to suss me out in a crowd.

But the little mind trick I have can either hide me from the public, or reveal me. Bringing out the eight-year-old in these eight cops turns them from taser-mad bullies into eight-year-old bullies and pranksters.

With tasers.

YouTube® — yeah, trademark as verb, sad, but true — "Starbucks® cop fight" to see the ensuing slapstick. These videos will make you laugh out loud, but avoid the ones with play-by-play; not a single one of those wags has comedic timing; none of those wags has the panache of Jim Robson or Danny Gallivan. (Some of you may have to consult the Google®; I'll wait.)

I lead Gramps from the store while the Keystone Cops (back to the Google® for you — my apologies) terrorize the customers and each other.

Gramps swats at my hand. "Whachu think you're doing?"

"You daft, man? I'm saving your ass from those cops."

"Why? I came to kill you."

"O, I know. You'll try again. Sometime in the future and sometime in the past. And maybe you could find a way to end me, but I doubt it."

"We all die eventually."

"Nope. Most of you die at some point, yes, but I don't."

"Why the hell not? What makes you so special?"

"Wish I knew. Wish I knew."

My theory involves a bit of hoodoo, a bit of cosmic history, a bit of Greek mythology, and works as well as any other theory. I figure my immortality was an accidental byproduct of the Big Bang. I, and others like me, are transformed tardigrades. Some more resilient than others, but each has a purpose, and once that purpose has overstayed its welcome, we fizzle and die, like the Greek gods, a narcissistic bunch who need the fear and adoration of the Greeks to live. Sure, they change their names and have brief second lives in early Rome before they fizzle out like the missus. But theory's just a fancy way of saying *guess*.

"I was. I am. I will be."

"Such a lame answer. You get that outta Genesis?"

"So what if I did? I wrote it."

"Yeah, right. I'm sure you believe you wrote it."

"Whatevs, dude. Listen, why don't you tell me what your beef is, and we can settle this at the bargaining table rather than battlefield?"

Okay, so the differences between battle and bargaining are negligible but almost no one dies at the bargaining table.

"You messed with my woman. You need to pay."

He has a point. But technically, I suppose, she messed with me and I let her. Since when is enjoying a hummer a crime? Anyway, I don't have the problem in his marriage, he does. He needs to work it out with her. He needs to stop busting my jaw. I would say I'm a lover, not a fighter but when you get right down to it, I suck at both.

"How bout I cut you a cheque? Name your price and I'll pay it."

"Ain't about the money."

"Seldom is. Seldom is. But money works like a poultice on all manner of hurt."

"Done talking yet?"

I could talk till he loses his will to live, but why risk him breaking the other side of my jaw, too. Funny how some things change with time, but the moments with Gramps and Granny Lanny remain the same, as if they share the Big Bang's significance. Perhaps they are my kryptonite. Up and down the timeline, he chases me. Up and down the timeline, I run and hide. What if fear of dying keeps me alive? What if I need Gramps and Granny Lanny to hold onto eternal life? My nemesis and my salvation, does it get any more Old Testament than this? Why risk it? I slip into two hours previous, take my flat white out onto Robson Street, and let the off-to-workers, next-great-novelists, students, street people, and children see me walking west.

Fun with time. Fun with perception. Fun with invisibility — of sorts. I allow the people at the Via Rail station to see me board the Squamish train. I allow the patrons at Whistler's The Flatulent Pig Inn see me. Search YouTube® (there, no verbing of the trademark this time; you happy?) for "snowboarding old guy shreds Black Mountain." The production values, although weak, show me at my best. Or do they? One of the videos captures me ripping a switch quadruple underflip 1620. Or does it? (Suck on that, Max Parrot. This old dude steals your trick and owns it. Or does he?)

Allowing images of me in snowy landscapes keeps Gramps scouring the north for the North Pole Homestead and toy factory.

Good luck with that one, Gramps.

From Squamish to Horseshoe Bay, where I pose with sixty "good little" girls and boys. Why do you diminish the value of your children like that? Fuck that *good little* bullshit; they're your children, not *little* pets you toss treats to every now and then.

Then Horseshoe Bay to Nanaimo. More pics with kids. The Google® catalogues over 100 million unique images of [The *real*] Santa[™] with over 100 million children. Saturating the internets with images of me keeps Gramps busy. It also keeps me busy during the offseason.

Fun is fun till someone loses a life.

November rains on mid- to north Vancouver Island will drown you if you stop moving. It might surprise you to learn that an old white dude resembling Santa can hitchhike and usually make better time than taking a bus. Not as fast as driving, and not nearly as quick as willing myself from one place to the next.

So from Nanaimo to Campbell River, not because I have to stop there, but because I like the place, and I can pose with more children. Two days in Campbell River, and then a five-hour slog to Port Hardy and Alert Bay. Only a day here. Icy rain. Threat of snow. Threat of rough seas. Twenty-four hours on the ferry to Prince Rupert. Another night to Juneau. A week in Juneau because word gets to Gramps that he will finds me there.

Imagine. If the naughty or nice list existed, I would have to cancel myself.

Once Gramps arrives here, he will trek to Denali, and traipse that snowscape for five months.

He doesn't know whether the government will strip him of his Indian status (again!) because he has spent so much of the last two years out of the country. He doesn't know whether the time out of the country is cumulative or resets every time he returns to Canada. Funny how a guy chasing you around the world and in and out of time will take the time to tell you what he fears. And will risk it just to cross me off. Well, try to, anyways.

Not once does he consider Granny Lanny may miss him, may need him at home. I can't read his mind, never could, but my informants provide data that my team of remote viewers and I parse. Cheesy, maybe, but it works, and so far has helped keep me alive.

Funny thing, an immortal fearing for their life, hey?

I don't know why Gramps holds onto his grudges. I keep telling him I am young then. Young and hot-headed. That *real* Santa™ makes our kids happy with his red suit, white beard, and the presents. Mainly the presents. No shortage of gonchies for them. And books. Them books make them curious. Ziff says, With my great cock, why'd you need to take that third one, from that filthy, old séme?? But That *real* Santa™'s tastes like peppermint sticks, and your puffs of dust don't taste that great, i'nit? I could lather mine up with sex shop stuff: almond, peppermint, vanilla, cinnamon, licorice. Whatever you like. I like maple smoked bacon. Everyone likes maple smoked bacon, and if you think I'm dipping my spaeks? in bacon grease for your pleasure, don't. Sick. Funny how my own husband don't want to talk about this one-night thing with That *real* Santa™. He would feel better if he showed me his anger. I'd feel better if he'd show his anger and stop spending most of his time searching the North Pole for That *real* Santa™'s house. Hell, I'd be mad and on him like an RCMP attack dog if I caught him with another woman. I'd beat him senseless and then I'd fix that woman so she won't mess around with any man ever again. Especially not mine. Makes no sense. Ziff sleeps with every woman he meets and I don't give a good goddamn, so long as he keeps his pecker clean. All he asks of a snag is that she's gotta pulse and wants to go. Between the two of them, I have one good man. It happens sometimes, I guess. Imagine spending eternity with two men you don't like. Imagine the lives of your thirteen children, had they lived their lives with parents who don't like or care for each other. Funny how Gramps has never googly-eyed babies into any other woman. He says he never even thought about it. He says that and I believe him. Maybe xeʔɬkʷúpiʔ has a plan for us because I can go to the janitor and fix him, but I can't marry Ziff instead, and I can't have fewer than my thirteen babies, and I can't protect my girls from that janitor. Thing is, would I really want to be married with Ziff? Aside from fucking good, he offers nothing, and will never give me my babies. If I marry with Ziff and still had Gramps' children, will either of them find happiness? Will I live in misery instead? I can only guess. Ziff asks, If you love him, why do you sleep around with me? Maybe I wouldn't fuck around with you at all — hee hee, I just love the way he cringes every time I say *fuck* — if Gramps spends more time at home than traipsing about the North Pole looking for That *real* Santa™. No! You say we belong together, why would you say something like that to me, Elaine? I keep telling you, never call me that. That's Mum's name, not mine. Sure, you, laugh like a little bitch now, but just you wait till you ask for a fuck. And how many times I gotta tell you I don't belong to no one? Not Gramps and certainly not you, Ziff. One shot's payback, two's overkill. Sometimes Ziff's a right royal a-hole. A clump of Ziff's hair falls out. Then another. His knees pop and crack and he groans as he gets up from the table. I don't feel too good. I know and it pains me to watch him disintegrate: another one of them things I'd change if I had the power. Get some rest, old man. Maybe you'll be better tomorrow. He says, Be best, woman. I'll be best. But he knows he won't be better or be best tomorrow. He knows we won't get on any better either. He dies in 117 days, losing a bit of himself every-damn-day till then: first his gorgeous hair; then his youthful beauty and sexual energy; then his godlike pheromones; then his memories. By the time he kicks the bucket, that hollow shell of a man resembles nothing of his former self. But who does? This he knows: he dies in 117 days and doesn't do a thing about it. Nothing. Maybe you should stop cheating time, Ziff. I chide, Maybe you could try to do something good for others, rather than just yourself. Woman, my life's a goddamn death sentence, so I live it up like I die in 117 days, cos it don't matter what I do. I accept that; so should you. If I stop messing with you, I might live longer, but it won't be much more time, if any. Look at all the women on my trapline. No man could give up on that much loving. Only men who think with their goddamn pricks, i'nit? Better than not thinking at all. You think? Ziff leaves, silent as a ghost. After brewing some green tea, I binge Netflix® cooking shows. Not that I ever try any of those recipes. A box of KD® with hot sauce and extra cheese and two slabs of SPAM®'s about as fancy as my cooking ever gets. If Gramps, the kids, or Ziff don't like it they can go ahead and eat in town. The grand-children never do; we always have at least six visit for dinner and games. But that Gramps just as sure as he's gonna spend half the goddamn year hunting That *real* Santa™, he's gonna bugger off into town for a chicken fried steak and eggs, a couple of pints and more stories and gossip than he'll hear at home. With the kids all grown and dead, and the grandchildren doting on us like overprotective parents, my husband ought to spend more time at home.

After three days' negotiations I have procurement and logistics deals with one more Chinese company. Fuck Amazon®. I will beat it at its own game.

Gladys, my sex doll, arrives. It looks like Granny Lanny and should sound like my missus. I pose it on the couch as nude as they sent her. They comped a naughty nurse, naughty nanny, naughty librarian, French maid (and all her implicit naughtiness), naughty Indian princess – the what now? – and school girls' outfits. What the actual fuck!? They must have expended their entire creative budget on getting the robot to work.

While torching the school girl outfits, I picture Granny Lanny and the missus in each of the others. No. No. No. And no. Not even. Can they not make a naughty costume that combines its illusion of sexiness with even a modicum of dignity?

Dignified and naughty? Naughtily dignified? Maybe sexy librarian, without the cheese? But naaaaaaaah; in the immortal words of Ralph Wiggum, "Unpossible!"

And nothing.

Lots and lots of nothing.

Plenty of nothing. When it comes to divining naughty alternatives, I shoot blanks.

So that sex doll wears a feather boa of dust and cat hair. And nothing more.

From across a dark room she almost looks alive, and sounds like a decent imitation of the missus. Like a '70s super stud, in a short, fluffy-fleece-edged silk robe, wide-open, and a bottle of Prosecco with two glasses in one hand, and a tube of lube in the other, I saunter to her. It.

It purrs, "You look exhausted, my lover. Would you like a back rub?"

I would, but it won't have that ability for another forty years or so. I will be here. This doll will not. It has a showroom stink to it, a new car smell.

Unlike the car, however, I don't want to take her — it — for a ride.

The manufacturer comped it so I might understand why requests for them have recently spiked. Almost as many women as men have added them to their Christmas wish lists. Mine, tricked out to the max, will pleasure me in a hundred different ways. It will respond to any sort of kiss I lay on her. Every gentle refusal led to another perk they added to the sponsorship package. I don't so much say yes, as I stop saying no. Their pitch had left me exhausted. Violated.

"Fine. I promise I will give it . . ."

"Please, call her Gladys. Calling her by her name helps suspend disbelief. Helps make the experience more immersive."

Whether I masturbate by hand, use a lotion sandwiched in a facecloth (my darling Fifi!), or use the robot, I am still masturbating.

"I will give it . . . her . . . Gladys, a go."

"You have made the right choice. We will honour your choice by upping your commission to twenty-five percent."

"Just leave it on the dresser before you leave."

"What?"

Harsh sigh. "Send over the contract and we'll go with your line of fuck-bots. Exclusively."

"Did my associate say twenty-five percent. She misspoke. Thirty-two percent. Yes, thirty-three percent for your generous endorsement."

Great, now the world has The *real* Santa™–approved fuck-bots. Christmas has reached an all-time low. But I stand to earn more from this fad than I do with the Cabbage Patch Kids back in the day. Mortals and their dolls. Part of me would like to change this aspect of my timeline. In 2019 I say no to the deal: "Christmas is for the kids. The kids. What would it look like if little Johnny races downstairs and the first thing he sees is a fuck-me toy?"

Now the imp in me wants to make a point, so I put a naked, provocatively posed Model-C, wearing only a plague mask beside the tree. This Model-C's cosmetics package resembles the wife/mother: either a $15,000 gag gift, or a way to keep her husband otherwise occupied. This little Johnny gambols down the stairs into the living room. "Mom? That you?"

"Call me Gisselle [the actual name of this little Johnny's mother], my handsome man. I'm yours. Do anything you want to me."

Here, the story could take an Oedipal twist, could traumatize little Johnny into lifelong therapy, or some other bizarre fate.

"Jeez, Mom! Take it back to your bedroom, you old perv."

"Yes, my man. Take me! Take me, now!"

"Take yourself." That trick will take effect in 2142. Bots of all kinds can climb stairs, run, jump, but cannot perform the task adequately, nor can they understand or appreciate the power of masturbation. In 2166, the sex-bots revolt.

Turmoil, unrest, and destructive distrust ensue.

In 2626 countries around the world follow the European Union's Proclamation 2626-8562-C, or the "Pleasure Bots are People Too" declaration, and recategorize sex-bots as people. Well, not people per se, but sentient, and masturbation remains an alien concept to them.

As I suspect, hubby's ordered the Model-C and plans to surprise the real Gisselle with the animatronic one. The wicked threesome he has envisioned fizzles from possible to not-at-all-likely when the real Gisselle meets her doppelgänger. She and little Johnny pack and leave before breakfast and after opening the boy's gifts. Hubby retires to his study with sex-bot Gisselle.

Gisselle raps on the study door and says, "I guess that's the next best thing to the Stepford wife you've always wanted."

Hubby stays quiet. Similar scenes play out around the world. Divorce rates soar. Bot porn floods the internet porn scene, unemploying millions of sex trade workers, alienating millions of spouses, partners, lovers.

Tinder for Bots® launches, and then Netflix for Bots®, where you rent a bot for a week at a time.

Sex-bot motels pop up in almost every city, town, and village.

Confidential clinics handling the sharp spike in STIs open up next to the motels. The W.H.O. declares *Neisseria gonorrhoeae anthropomorphisus,* better known as Bot Clap, a pandemic. Total global deaths top seven million before world leaders and (mostly) men consider the pandemic more than a simple, regional outbreak.

The usual loons spout the same loony lies and conspiracy theories since the first great plague back in Egypt's heydays.

Maybe older. I didn't start paying attention until the Black Plague and its town criers downplaying its seriousness even as carts filled with the dead and mostly dead creeped past them in the high streets, low streets, middle streets. Same lies. Similar nouns and verbs. Different costumes. Different delivery methods. But the same lies and similar language.

Of course *real* people revolt. Women the loudest. (I suspect most men wanted to keep their "little secret," or feared everyone would think their loud voices compensated for their tiny members.) Governments around the world tell the women they hear them; they will investigate. They will strike Royal Commissions into the matter. The Commissions only have the power to report on this new degradation of people, mostly women, and provide guidelines.

Governments make token attempts at fulfilling the guidelines. But fully embracing these changes costs more than we can reasonably expect to add to our taxes. So they fund additional studies, each one with a narrower scope than the one before it.

Surveys say that male sex-bots play companion roles, especially for people with pet allergies, do not want or like pets, or live in buildings where pets are banned.

Yeah, I believe that.

A $15,000 dildo, a $15,000 vibrator, unless employed as a status symbol, works just as well as a forty-dollar one from Amazon®. But don't buy it from them. Mine sell for $39.95 and you don't need to subscribe to a premium feature for free delivery.

I put a glass in front of it . . . her, erm, Gladys . . . tip the bottle at the doll, and drink from it. Slam the empty down. "Would you like another? No? Well don't mind if I do."

Because I don't want to live in this world, I take the deal, and give my Model-A sex-bot-Gladys a home. Dressed in a hazmat suit and armed with a baseball bat, she stands by the front door. Her forever home.

So the story could end here, me in my nihilistic misery and Gramps in his ancient rage and Granny Lanny in her I-don't-know-what. A nice ambiguous ending, a what-the-fuck-have-I-just-read ending.

I don't know about you, but that feels gimmicky and cheap.

So I face Gramps deep inside a Mendenhall ice cave. I know his moves as well as he. We dance as we've danced countless times before, and will, countless times then. He swings and never misses and I take every blow, awaiting the one that will terminate the loop, ending this crazy dance for all time.

It seems I've thought this thought before. A time or two. In each iteration of these final moments, I want time to end, despite the fact it will destroy every living creature and every written and oral history. And I tell myself: The planet deserves this. The universe deserves this. I am doing us all a favour. A huge favour.

Gramps' hands close around my neck. I go woozy.

Darkness folds us into her spidery web.

Once again.

Once.

A.

Fucking.

Gain.

Here. Tumbling through time toward the end of everything with Gramps on me like a rabid wolverine: past, present, future, and each alternate reality, each parallel universe, each cosmic thread, each cosmic being. The cataclysmic slorp (I wish the universe instead would implode with a Gib Gnab) of the universe sucking itself back into its own navel rises and falls underneath and above the chorus of a gazillion languages screaming in unison: "Aww fuck, not again. Not again. Please, no, not again."

In space, no one can hear you beg.

Then the nothing: a blackness without heat or cold.

Without breadth.

Without depth.

Without height.

Without time.

Without space.

Gramps' hands tight around my throat, choking the life from me, and it would leave, had it somewhere to go. And he stops, all slack-jawed, and horks — not a loogey — but a smugging, top-hatted tardigrade on a bulbous pool-toy swan. Its four legs crossed, a piña colada in one hand, and it tips its blue velvet top hat with the other and floats away. And Gramps' grip loosens and he says, "Huh. That's new."

And I croak, "Hmmm. Maybe this is the end? The end, at last!?"

Gramps grunts and recloses my throat, and says, "Why don't you die, dammit?"

He can't choke out the air, but my words have nowhere to go except to burn to death in my gut's pool of hydrochloric acid.

BA

NG

Acknowledgements

Kʷukʷscémxʷ to these folks for publishing some of the stories in their journals and the anthology. Also, many thanks to the readers and judges who selected some of these stories for prizes or short- and longlists:

2021 "SPAM® Stew and the MALM Minimalist Bedroom Set from IKEA®," in *Food of Our People*, Exile Editions, Summer 2021.
2021 "Sunshine Rainbow Peace Ranch," *Prairie Fire*, Spring 2020.
2020 "Three Bucks," *FreeFall*, 30.2, Fall 2020.
2020 "Roạdkill," *The Antigonish Review*, 199.
2020 "ball lightnin," *The Antigonish Review*, 199.

2021 CBC Short Story Contest longlist for "Splatter Pattern."
2018 Prism International Jacob Zilber Prize for Short Fiction shortlist for "A Wager."

Kʷukʷscémxʷ, Néxʷm kʷukʷscéyp ʔes kncémxʷ (Thank You, Thank You Very Much)!

Kʷukʷscémxʷ, Susan; you make it possible for me to write.

Kʷukʷscémxʷ, Kelsey and the board and staff at Freehand for taking a chance on *Tales*.

Kʷukʷscémxʷ, Jamie. Editing *Tales* while getting *River, Diverted* ready for publication, and then touring it, must've been tough. I appreciate your guidance and help in shaping the final manuscript.

Kʷukʷscémxʷ, Shelagh Rogers, Carol Rose GoldenEagle, and Susan Holbrook for agreeing to blurb *Tales*.

Kʷukʷscémxʷ, Shelagh, for advocating Indigenous writers and writing on The Next Chapter since 2008, and for making Saturdays great again.

Kʷukʷscémxʷ, Susan Holbrook, for your kind, quiet inspiration, and encouragement in shaping this project. I couldn't have asked for a better academic advisor.

Kʷukʷscémxʷ, Sandra Muse Isaacs and Nicholas Papador, for agreeing to sit as readers on my thesis defence.

Kʷukʷscémxʷ, Karl Jirgens, for introducing me to Harry Robinson's stories, and Thomas King's brilliant essay "Godzilla vs Post-Colonial," and showing me the breadth and depth of Indigenous Canadian writing.

Kʷukʷscémxʷ, Danielle, Renée, Doug, and André. Your work and your critiques keep me striving to write better.

Kʷukʷscémxʷ, Thomas King, your work, from *Dead Dog Café*, through the Thumps DreadfulWater mysteries has given me hours and hours of pleasure, and opened my mind and heart to contemplate Story, and the state of NDNcountry.

Kʷukʷscémxʷ, Harry Robinson! Your vision, your voice, your stories amaze.

Kʷukʷscémxʷ, Wendy Wickwire; your love of story shows in the careful way you transcribed Robinson's stories. And the world's a little better because of it.

Kʷukʷscémxʷ, to my family: the Swites of Westbank First Nation via Deadman's Creek; the Earls, the Thomases, the Dixons, and the Peterses of Lytton and Hope and Merritt and Kamloops; especially my tough, resilient, and devoted — with a heart as big as NDNcountry — baby sis, Lisa.

Kʷukʷscémxʷ, also, to the səmséme? branch, the global Grisenth-waite clan who started as boar breeders in England's lake district.

Kʷukʷscémxʷ, Cat, Bitsy, or Hobbitt-zee-Cat. I had no idea I wanted or needed a cat in my life, but since you invited yourself into our home and decided to stay, home feels a little homier. Love your constant humming, your propensity for flashing a Zoom audience, the way you relax so profoundly that you sometimes roll off the window ledge, and your way of breaking the flow of my writing by demanding a scritch, a hug, or food. Usually food.

Afterword

Okay. So this book started life as my graduate thesis in Creative Writing. I had no idea I had these stories in me, until my thesis advisor Susan Holbrook gently coaxed them from me. I worried that I only had one writing voice, Squito Bob's, the narrator of almost every short story I'd written prior to returning to school (University of Windsor) in 2015, and the novel *Home Waltz*, part of which I workshopped in Nino Ricci's undergrad novel writing class.

Now, as much as I love Squito and his stories and his narrative voice, I feared it might devolve into self-parody if I tried to make a career of it. And I feared Squito's voice and Squito's stories had spent my whole literary load. Ah, anxiety, how you've complicated my life!

Now Squito came to life in response to W.P. Kinsella's Hobbema stories. At first, they entertained and amused me. And by the end of the third collection I read, the stories angered me. I saw them as so not anything like my experience as an urbanized nłeʔkepmx teen/man. And out popped angry and lost Squito. His voice was so fully formed that when I read a Squito story aloud, it came out in rez voice. And I had no idea. I didn't hear it as I read — mind you, the anxiety blocked out everything except my place on the page. But an audience member asked whether I knew my accent changed as I read, and I said no, because, why lie?

Since then, I consciously work on the accent. And sometimes it feels disingenuous. And sometimes it doesn't.

Then, in Karl Jirgens' Indigenous Literature class, we studied Thomas King's brilliant 1990 essay, "Godzilla vs. Post-Colonial." King's *A Short History of Indians in Canada,* notably the titular story, had already hit me hard. I loved the way he told the story. How a story so short could take years to unpack. Back in the '80s I read an essay analyzing Roch Carrier's "The Hockey Sweater," an equally short story to King's, that was at least three times the length of the story. Now, had I the intellectual capacity to write that thoughtfully on any literary work, I might deep dive into many of King's fictions.

As it is, however, I write fiction. I write stories. I think stories. I dream stories. And in order to understand King's concept of the interfusional style of Indigenous literatures — as described in "Godzilla" — I tried to write in the interfusional style. I suppose I should mention that interfusional stories blend both oral and written literary traditions. King credits Harry Robinson with its invention.

And here, I must digress and regale you with a bit of Robinson's story, as told by his editor/compiler, Wendy Wickwire, in the introduction to *Write It on Your Heart: The Epic World of an Okanagan Storyteller:*

> More than anything, Harry laments the erosion of his native language, and the replacement of storytelling by television and radio. In the Similkameen Valley, English is rapidly replacing the Okanagan language. In Harry's view, he is one of the last of the old storytellers. "I'm going to disappear," he says, "and there will be no more telling stories."
>
> As more and more of his listeners, natives [sic] included, understood only English, Harry began telling his old stories in English to keep them alive. By the time I [Wickwire] met him in 1977, he had become as skilled a storyteller in English as he had been in his native tongue.

Now Wickwire had been recording Robinson' stories for years, and suggested that some of them might belong in a book. And Robinson loved the idea. As Wickwire writes, "It was one way to leave his people with this testament to their past."

Some of the stories in *Heart* also belong to the nɬeʔkepmx. And that fact fills me with joy. But the real joy bubbles up in their reading. Robinson and Wickwire ensured that each story looked on the page as it did on the ear. As King notes, the stories come to life when read aloud. My story "Snk̓y̓ép and His Shiny New Choker" was inspired by Thomas King's collections *A Short History of Indians in Canada* and *One Good Story, That One.* And I attempted to inhabit his voice and style. The exercise helped me better understand interfusionality.

So my wish is that you will revisit some of these twelve stories and read them aloud. Not necessarily in rez voice, unless it comes naturally to you, of course. See if reading aloud changes your feelings, or alters your understanding of them.

Some of these stories arrived in dreams. Some, "Spatter Pattern" for instance, were suggested by characters from Squito's stories. Me-Who-Looks-At-Me had bullied himself into an early draft of *Home Waltz* and radically changed the story. I destroyed that draft. It was evil! Me-Who-Looks-At-Me premiered in the National Magazine Award finalist story "How Mosquito Got His Name." He was inspired, in part, by Graham Greene's character in *Clearcut*. Me-Who-Looks-At-Me isn't, however, a trickster figure. But I suppose you could read him that way.

"The Sunshine Rainbow Peace Ranch" was inspired by Kinsella's "First Names and Empty Pockets," where Janis Joplin lives past age twenty-seven. As a kid I went through a brief period where I wanted to be Jim Morrison. I mean, kids think the darnedest things, right? So I asked the question, "What if Jim Morrison didn't die in Paris 3 July 1971, and instead arrived at Smallton — the town/landscape shared by the characters in these stories and Squito's — the next day, with a posse of thirty or so friends?" My initial story had Morris Jim, his clever nom de guerre, speak mostly in lines of Morrison's poetry. The potential for legal challenges put the kibosh on that. And finding the appropriate responses proved tricky. So I immersed myself in Morrison's poems, both written and orated. I think I've succeeded in making Morris Jim speak like Jim Morrison.

"SPAM® Stew and the MALM Minimalist Bedroom Set from IKEA®" was borne of panic. Exile, the publisher of *Food of My People*, an anthology of recipe-based stories, called me up and asked if I had a food-related story. He needed it in two days. I said sure thing, despite the fact that I had no food stories. But I had happy memories of my Grandpa Dave, who loved SPAM® stew. The ranch had no power or water, so no refrigeration. SPAM® was our bologna. And he loved Tabasco®. I couldn't find yéye?'s recipe. None of my cousins had it. So I invented the recipe, even bought two cans of SPAM® and made an edible stew. I don't know whether Grandpa Dave would have liked it, but his fictional persona loved it enough to rise from his grave to eat with yéye? and two of his kids (note: this is an alternate version of Squito's family). And I ground out the story in two days. Two very long, stressful days.

Stories such as "Roadkill" and "Three Bucks" are based on stories I heard around the backyard bonfire when I was a kid. And the way I initially heard the one about the bucks, the storyteller, hunting with a semi-automatic, squeezed off three rounds with one pull, and each bullet nailed a different buck. Far more logical, and probable than Miracle Johnny's version. But his name is Miracle. So . . .

"ball lightnin" is based on one of the only stories my grandmother Margaret ever told about her childhood in Lytton. I've no recollection of most of the story's details, so I reinvented it. The only image that stuck is that scared little girl running for her life. It was enough.

Now "Gramps vs The *real* Santa™" was an idea based loosely on the Christmas song "I Saw Mommy Kissing Santa Claus." And an idea alone — good or not-so-good — isn't strong enough to carry a story. It was initially on the list of stories for my thesis project. It didn't make the final draft. "SPAM® Stew" took only two very long days to write, with minor edits afterwards. "Gramps" took the better part of three years to complete. Its edits have been relatively minor. And it's not your regular sort of story. I suppose you could label it experimental, a death knell to readers such as me. At various times over the years I have read Douglas Adams, Richard Brautigan, Grant Naylor, and Tom Robbins, whose *Still Life With Woodpecker* remains one of my all-time favourite books. I suspect their influences helped shape this story. Come to think of it, Lewis Carroll's *Alice's Adventures in Wonderland* may have influenced "Gramps" too.

Anyways, kʷukʷscémxʷ; néxʷm kʷukʷscéyp ʔes kncémxʷ for reading.

Gord is nłeʔkepmx, a member of the Lytton First Nation, and has earned an MA in English Literature & Creative Writing at the University of Windsor (2020). His first novel, *Home Waltz*, a finalist for the 2021 Governor General's Award for fiction, is now available.

His work has appeared in *Prairie Fire*, *FreeFall*, *Exile Quarterly*, *The Antigonish Review*, *Our Stories Literary Journal*, *Prism International*, *ndnCountry*, *Offset 17*, *Bawaajigan: Stories of Power*, and *Food of My People*. His work has earned a number of prizes, including the 2013 John Kenneth Galbraith Literary Award.